Praise For The Fiery Tales

"Evocative, erotic. . . [A] sensual treat!"
— **Sylvia Day**,
#1 *New York Times* bestselling author

"Hot enough to warm the coldest winter night."
— **Publishers Weekly**

"Sophisticated and deeply romantic."
—**Elizabeth Hoyt**,
New York Times bestselling author

"Sure to delight!"
— **Jennifer Ashley**,
New York Times bestselling author

"The most luscious, sexy take on classic fairy tales I've ever read!"
—**Cheryl Holt**,
New York Times bestselling author

"Sets the classic fairy tale(s) ablaze!"
—**Anna Campbell**,
bestselling, award-winning author

The Lovely Duckling

A Fiery Tale

LILA DIPASQUA

DiPasqua

Excerpt from *The Princess and the Diamonds*, in *The Princess in His Bed* anthology by Lila DiPasqua copyright © Lila DiPasqua
Cover: Carrie Divine/Seductive Designs

Photography of couple: © Period Images;

Interior Design by Woven Red Author Services, www.WovenRed.ca

PRINTING HISTORY
First Edition: From *The Princess in His Bed*, Berkley Sensation/Penguin Group (USA) Inc.—November 2010
Second Edition: Lila DiPasqua—December, 2016

ISBN: 978-0-9951655-5-7 (trade pbk)
ISBN: 978-0-9951655-4-0 (e-book)

To anyone who was ever made to feel like an ugly duckling.

May you show them all that you're a swan.

CHAPTER ONE

*An "ugly duckling" is someone who blossoms
beautifully after an unpromising beginning.*
—Eric Donald Hirsch et al., *The New Dictionary
of Cultural Literacy*, 2002

France, 1683

"*Details*, Vincent. You cannot simply state you had two women
last night without offering *details*," Gilbert complained, sporting
his usual lazy smile.

Joseph d'Alumbert, Marquis de Valle, rose from his plush
chair and strode across the floral carpet over to the window in
the antechamber—away from his twin brother Vincent and
younger brother Gilbert. He knew full well Vincent wasn't about
to withhold a single salacious detail of his evening of excess.

He simply wanted their younger brother to beg a little.

"Ah, the details . . ." Without turning around, Joseph knew
his twin was grinning. He heard it in his tone. Though he and
his brothers ordinarily shared the particulars of their carnal encounters, at the moment, Joseph didn't care a whit how Vincent's
evening had unfolded.

He was on edge. Worse, since his arrival yesterday at the Comtesse de Saint-Arnaud's country estate, he found himself looking out the window at the courtyard one too many times.

And here he was. Doing it *again*.

Joseph braced his hands on the window frame as he gazed down at the empty cobblestone courtyard. It was late afternoon. The Comtesse's week-long masqueraded affair was into its second day. Well under way. *She's not coming*, he mentally willed.

"Well?" Gilbert prompted Vincent, impatience in his tone.

"He had the d'Esseur sisters, Gilbert," Joseph responded for his twin. "There's nothing new there. Everyone has fucked them."

"I haven't!" Gilbert said. "How were they, Vincent? How can you be certain it was them? Everyone's identity is disguised."

Vincent chuckled. "Dear brother, you have been away in the campaign too long. Marie and Jeanne d'Esseur are known for two things. Their talented mouths. And their unfortunate, distinctive laugh . . ."

The Comtesse's parties were never short on decadent diversions—to suit just about any taste. Yet last eve, instead of indulging in some debauchery of his own, Joseph had spent it in the company of the Comtesse's fine brandy. Unable to focus on the amusements at hand, he'd actually turned down women who were eager to engage in just the sort of impersonal sex he preferred.

His thoughts were being pulled toward a female who wasn't even in attendance.

"Fine. Wonderful. They had a distinctive laugh," Gilbert said. "What else, Vincent? Out with it. Tell me before I stop asking altogether."

At that, Vincent laughed. "We both know you won't," he needled Gilbert. "But since you *insist*, I shall tell you . . . I had them in the gardens, behind the statue of Zeus . . ."

A black carriage pulled into the courtyard, capturing Joseph's attention. His brothers' voices immediately faded into the distance as he watched it halt before the main doors of the Comtesse's château. Sunshine glinted off its top.

He tensed.

Moments later, a figure alighted with the aid of the footman. She wore a mask. And a wig. But it didn't matter. It was *her*. He'd know her anywhere. The way she was dressed—the multiple layers of fabrics—made him certain.

Merde.

He'd hoped he'd convinced her to stay away. He knew exactly what she was after. Her letter had stated it plainly. She was here for the same reason everyone attended the Comtesse's gatherings.

For the carnal entertainment.

For anonymous sex.

Joseph tightened his jaw and held back the expletives thundering in his head. He wasn't about to let his brothers know how discomposed this woman had him. He'd never live it down. Women didn't normally stir him beyond the physical. Yet lately Emilie de Sarron had been affecting him on a number of disquieting levels.

Jésus-Christ, she didn't belong here. Not with this group. At hand were the very people who had driven her into seclusion ten years ago.

He was among the guilty.

He'd been a party to her humiliation the night Emilie had been introduced into society. As son of the Duc de Vernant, Joseph hadn't made it a habit to take stock of his behavior. He'd always done as he pleased. Behaved as he willed, without thought or concern. Without excuses or apologies. But the hurt he'd seen in her soft green eyes before she turned and left was still vivid in his mind. Still ate at his conscience. Even after a decade.

She'd withdrawn from society after that night.

She was never betrothed. Never married. He'd never seen her again until last year when he spotted her at the theater. And she looked beautiful; her pale-colored hair and light-colored eyes had always been a stunning combination. Yet the many layers of clothing she wore were a sobering reminder of what made Emilie different from everyone else.

Driven by a need to know how she'd fared all these years, Joseph had sent her a letter the day after the theater. He never imagined she'd be so delightfully witty. Refreshingly frank. Surprisingly bold.

A year later he was still corresponding with her.

The more he got to know the real Emilie, the more he liked her. And the worse he felt for the impact he'd had on her life. A life that might have turned out very different had the incident ten years ago not occurred.

But he couldn't change the past no matter how much he wished it.

Emilie was the only one to affect his conscience, when his conscience had never bothered him before. She was the only one to inspire a troubling sense of possessiveness. Or a level of interest he didn't normally offer women.

Limiting the women in his life to bed sport, the rapport he had with this particular female was novel. He'd never touched her, never tasted her, yet he knew her more intimately than any woman he'd ever bedded. Emilie was restless, looking for a reprieve from her staid existence. She longed for a bit of gaiety. She was starved for a taste of passion.

And she was intent on using the anonymity the masquerade offered to disguise her identity, in order to sample some.

Just imagine the stir it would cause if the Comtesse's guests were to learn Emilie de Sarron was back. After ten years of self-imposed exile.

"Are you listening to anything I'm saying?" Vincent's voice cut through his thoughts. Joseph reluctantly pulled his attention away from the window.

His twin approached, stopped beside him, and looked down at the courtyard. "Well, well. A new lady has arrived. Do you know who she is?"

"No," Joseph lied.

Gilbert moved to the window and studied Emilie as she spoke to the footman. "What difference does it make who she is?" He grinned. "Someone new to play with."

An objection shot up Joseph's throat. He swallowed it back down.

He'd no right to object. Emilie was free to have sex with whomever she chose. This was something she wanted, and he wasn't going to interfere in any way. He'd offered his concerns about her intentions. Clearly, she'd chosen to proceed nonetheless. He had no idea how badly she'd been burned as an infant, but that fire had changed her life forever, scarring her body permanently. Scars she kept hidden beneath her clothing.

Just how easily a man would detect them during sex, he'd no clue. Her injuries were one of the few topics they had never touched upon in their letters.

The one thing he knew for certain was that *he* wasn't going to be the one deflowering her. No matter how stirring her latest letters—filled with sexual curiosity and sensual yearnings—had been.

He'd done enough to her already.

If she felt confident she could indulge in an amorous encounter without anyone identifying her or discovering her scars, then that should put an end to his disquiet.

But it didn't.

The idea of her giving herself to one or more of the men in attendance was actually plaguing him, and he had no idea why it should.

If that weren't bad enough, he had another problem. A sizable one.

Emilie had given him her trust, something he knew she didn't offer just anyone.

And he was lying to her.

Knowing she wouldn't correspond with him if he'd used his name, he'd misled her in his first letter when he'd inquired about her wellbeing. And in every letter since. Emilie de Sarron believed that the man she'd opened herself to, confided her most intimate thoughts and longings to—was his brother Vincent.

Joseph was too far into this now. To reveal his deception would only hurt her terribly and that was something he couldn't bring himself to do to her. Not again.

Somehow, some way he had to get through the rest of the masquerade without Emilie—or Vincent—discovering his lie.

Just how the bloody hell was he going to maintain the ruse *here?*

Emilie stepped around the footman and walked into the château. Joseph turned on his heel and snatched up his mask. "There is a party under way. I'm off." He marched out of the room without a look back.

Gilbert turned to Vincent. "Well? Shouldn't we join in?"

Vincent glanced down at the courtyard, noting the woman was gone. He smiled good-naturedly. "Absolutely. I believe the first thing I'm going to do is acquaint myself with the newly arrived lady."

*****

"You're here!" Beaming, Pauline de Naylon, Comtesse de Saint-Arnaud, stepped around the desk in her library toward Emilie, her arms wide open.

Removing her demi-mask, Emilie smiled at her aunt, hoping she didn't look as nervous as she felt. Her heart had pounded the entire trip from her townhouse in the city to the Comtesse's country estate. The closer she got to the Comtesse's château, the more she wrestled with her courage. What she was doing was daring. Risky. A tad foolhardy. She'd purposely distanced herself from many of the guests in attendance and their vicious tongue-wagging years ago.

It took everything she had not to turn and run back into hiding.

Pauline embraced her warmly and pressed her cheek to hers. "I'm delighted you came."

"Hrrmph." Twenty years Emilie's senior, her cousin Marthe d'Arbac, Marquise de Sere, scowled from the doorway. She'd all but dragged her feet from the Comtesse's main doors to the library. "Your invitation has drawn her into the Den of Iniquity. What is there to be delighted about?"

"Ah, Marthe." Pauline's smile faded. Her tone was flat. "You made the trip, too. It was lovely of you to accompany Emilie. Feel free to take your leave at any time." Pauline looped arms with Emilie. "She's in good hands now."

Marthe lifted her chin a notch and clasped her hands before her. Emilie sensed it was likely to keep herself from strangling Pauline. The two women had maintained an unwavering animosity, stemming from their court battle where Marthe and her husband, the late Marquis de Sere, had won guardianship of Emilie as a child and control over her vast fortune until she came of age—years ago. Pauline from her mother's side and Marthe from her father's side of the family, the only things they had in common were their age, their widowhood, and their affection for Emilie.

Marthe's eyes narrowed. "I'll not abandon Emilie in this . . . place. It's utterly shocking what you allow in your home. Public fornication."

Emilie sighed. "Marthe, that will be quite en—"

"I allow private fornication as well," Pauline said. "Perhaps if you had a man more often, Marthe, you wouldn't be quite so shocked."

Emilie mentally cringed. A battle was afoot.

Just as expected, Marthe fired back. "Oh, you . . . ! You are utterly brazen! You see what I mean, Emilie? She is shameless. She always has been. We should get back in the carriage and return home immediately."

"She has been cloistered long enough!" Pauline countered, releasing Emilie's arm. She pointed an accusatory finger at

Marthe. "You are to blame. You and that horrible late husband of yours—"

Emilie took a deep breath, striving for patience. The last thing she needed was bickering between her kin. Her nerves were far too frayed. She'd come looking for a break from the monotony in her life. But this wasn't the sort of entertainment she had in mind.

Both women meant the world to her.

If she hadn't wanted Marthe and Pauline to repair their rift, she'd have left Marthe behind, given Emilie's carnal intent. Perhaps it was too ambitious to plan on enjoying a lover and bringing Marthe and Pauline together after all this time, hoping they'd finally make peace.

Emilie held up a hand to silence them and implored, "Enough. Both of you. Please. Darling Aunt Pauline, you simply must attempt to be nice to Marthe."

Pauline crossed her arms. "She doesn't make it easy. She's entirely too single-minded and obstinate."

Marthe sucked in a sharp breath, indignant. Emilie walked over and placed an arm around her. Giving her an affectionate squeeze, she quickly stemmed Marthe's flow of hot words. "Qualities you both share at times, no?" she asked, looking pointedly at both women.

Marthe clamped her mouth shut and looked away. Pauline simply studied the state of the nails on her left hand. Both refused to admit the truth.

Taking advantage of the silence, Emilie continued. "Now then, we've discussed this," she said to Marthe. "I'll not be dissuaded. I'm seeing this through. If you don't wish to stay, you may leave. I shall see you at home in a week."

"But Emilie . . ." Marthe said. "What you're planning to do . . . You're actually contemplating your own ruin. You don't belong here. You are not like these women."

Those words had bite, though Emilie knew they were innocently dealt.

She smoothed a hand down her cloak. It was summer. A cloak wasn't needed, but she wore one anyway. She owned several, various colors, various fabrics. Heavy to light. Ornate to plain. For every season. The more she covered her body, the more confidence she had. It was something she'd done since she was a child. It hadn't stopped the ridicule. Nothing ever had.

It gave her a certain comfort to envelope herself within the coverings of fabric. A barrier between her and the outside world.

But she was tired of the way she lived.

Tired of living vicariously through the characters in the books she read, the theater she frequented on occasion, and the precious few friends she corresponded with.

Tired of not really living at all.

Her discontent had become so deep, it had dragged her out of her safe solitary existence straight into one of the Comtesse's notorious masquerades. "You are correct. I am not like these women. Or any woman. Thanks to the scars," she said. "And no amorous encounter could bring about my ruin. My ruin happened long ago in a fire that took the lives of my parents and left me in this rather sorry—unmarriageable—state."

Marthe lowered her head, clearly remorseful of her words.

"Love and marriage are beyond my reach. I've made my peace with that," Emilie said. "But I refuse to live out my life without ever knowing a taste of passion."

As long as it was real and as scintillating as the passion she'd read about.

"If passion is what you want, then that is exactly what you shall have, ma chère," Pauline said. "Besides, marriage is highly overrated. Trust me, I should know. I was married to the Comte de Saint-Arnaud. A lover is much more preferable than a husband. You can easily change a lover."

Marthe's head shot up. "Have you no decency?"

"Oh, hush, Marthe." Pauline walked up to Emilie and pulled her away from her older cousin. "You are going to enjoy yourself this week."

"But—But—what if they recognize her?" Marthe asked.
"You know what they did years ago—"

"No one will recognize me," Emilie cut her off abruptly, not
wanting to remember that night. Or talk about it. She knew
Marthe meant well. Unlike her husband, the Marquis de Sere,
who had been more interested in Emilie's inheritance than in
her, Marthe was genuinely concerned for her welfare. "After
such a lengthy absence, no one will think for a moment that I'd
be in attendance. Besides, everyone wears masks at all times and
even costumes. Isn't that so?" she asked Pauline. Her layered
mode of dress wouldn't look odd here.

"Yes. The ladies especially. They make every effort to maintain their anonymity—with both elaborate masks and outfits. I
find men don't make as much of an effort to conceal their iden-
tities, but they, too, wear the required mask. And no one, absolutely no one, is permitted to unmask anyone here. However, if
during a carnal encounter, in a private setting, one chooses to
reveal oneself, then that is between the lovers at play."

Marthe slapped her hands over her ears. "I can't listen to
this."

Pauline's smile broadened at Marthe's discomfort. "There are
plenty of men here to choose from, Emilie. Many of them were
not there that horrible night."

Pauline's response made Emilie's heart flutter. There was a
very special man somewhere in the Comtesse's home, one who
wasn't part of that incident a decade ago.

Vincent d'Alumbert.

He'd mentioned in his letter that he, too, would be in attendance at the masquerade. She'd only ever seen him once, a long,
long time ago. She was so eager to see him again and in person.
More than she could ever admit. Probably more than she should.

But she couldn't help having tender feelings for him. He and
his letters were a source of joy. She felt so very close to him,
having forged a connection with him she'd never had with anyone else. There was nothing she couldn't ask him. Or tell him.
And she'd divulged plenty.

Given what she was attempting to do—indulge in debauchery—it settled her nerves just knowing he'd be present. On hand to offer advice if she needed it.

Pauline donned her silver-colored demi-mask with white plumes, then approached and placed her hands on Emilie's shoulders. Looking her firmly in the eye, she asked, "Are you absolutely certain you want to do this?"

Emilie tamped down her fears and self-doubt and steeled her courage. "Yes." Just once she wanted to be desired. For the next few days, she was going to step into the world of make-believe. With the aid of her masks, be transformed into someone else. For the first time ever, she wasn't going to be looked at as a misfit. Or damaged. She wouldn't be Emilie Embers. Or Singed de Sarron. Or equally as detestable, The Ugly Little Duckling— cruel names she'd endured all her life.

She deserved to be wanted. Kissed. Touched. Held. Every woman did, no matter her plight.

"Very well. Then let us begin." Pauline took Emilie's demi-mask of gold and red from her hand and tied it in place. "There's no time like the present." Looping her arm with Emilie's once again, she led her to the door. "You don't have to worry about approaching the men. They'll no doubt approach you."

CHAPTER TWO

The Comtesse opened the library door.

Sounds of chatter and gaiety rushed up to Emilie. Her pulse quickened. In the tapestry-lined hallway, groupings of people were clustered about, the throng in attendance having swelled into the corridor.

Be brave now. You are going to do this.

Nothing was going to ruin this for her. Certainly not the people who'd ruined what was to be a special night ten years ago. This time would be different. She'd made certain of it. She'd taken every precaution. Thought the plan through, contemplating every foreseeable scenario.

She had a strong feeling this was going to be a week she'd never forget.

The crowd shifted. A couple across the hallway caught Emilie's attention. A gentleman in a bright yellow justacorps had a woman pinned against the wall as she willingly, eagerly participated in a heated, most ravenous kiss. So engrossed in each other, they were completely unaware of anything else. Or anyone else.

Imagine having a man that hungry for you, Emilie . . . The wistful thought echoed in the empty chambers inside her heart.

She'd spent too many nights lying in her empty bed picturing it . . . wondering what it would be like with a very specific, potently appealing man.

But that man was a dear friend. And he'd never think of her in that way or desire her like that.

"Madame . . . Mademoiselle . . ." A male voice interrupted her thoughts. She dragged her gaze away from the lovers to the gentleman standing before her.

Her breath lodged in her throat. Though he wore a demi-mask, she recognized his tall, sculpted form immediately. And especially those vivid blue eyes . . . A distinct d'Alumbert family trait.

"Good afternoon." His voice was smooth, rich, masculine, as he addressed both her and her aunt with a slight bow. "Would you care to join me for a walk?" He held out his hand to Emilie.

"Wait!" Marthe's protest came from inside the library. Her rapid footsteps quickly approaching were met with the slam of the library door as Pauline swung her foot back and kicked it shut behind her. Closing Marthe inside the room.

"Of course she'd like to join you," Pauline said and gave Emilie a slight shove in the man's direction.

The next thing she knew, Emilie's hand was tucked into his arm, and he was leading her down the hallway. She was swallowed into the crowd. Her mind raced. She had no idea where they were going. But one thing was certain—this was one of the Duc de Vernant's twin sons.

But which one? They were identical.

She'd told Vincent in her letter she'd have on a yellow silk cloak. In all likelihood this was him, but she couldn't blurt out his name. Worse, she couldn't shake the feeling that this wasn't her dear friend. Every fiber of her being screamed, *"It's Joseph!"* She began to quiver and quake, her ire mountaining by the moment as the very memory she'd fought for years to forget materialized in her mind. Joseph's vibrant blue eyes mocking her. His cruel laughter as he joined in with the others that horrid night echoed in her ears. The lash of their malicious tongues had cut deep.

And still stung after all this time no matter how hard she'd tried to forget it.

She loathed everything about the older twin.

A self-indulgent roué. Coldhearted. Arrogant and callous to the core. There was nothing appealing about Joseph d'Alumbert. He bore none of the fine qualities Vincent had. The mere thought of Joseph touching her filled her with rage. With outrage. With stomach-churning revulsion.

They'd reached the grand staircase, and he was beginning to lead her up the stairs. She'd gone no farther than the second step when she yanked her hand away as if it burned, surprising him with her action.

"I know it's against the rules, but I'll need your name before we proceed," she said, amazed her voice didn't quiver, alerting him to her discomposure. If this was Joseph, she'd feign a malady and remove herself from his distasteful presence. Posthaste.

He glanced past her and scanned the crowded vestibule, then returned his gaze to hers. A slow grin formed on his far-too-attractive mouth and he leaned in. "It is against the rules," he said softly in her ear. "And it is me, Vincent."

Joseph pulled back and was immediately bedazzled by the sheer radiance of Emilie's smile. Beguiling green eyes—a combination of innocent sensuality—stared back at him through her mask, mirroring her content. He felt his insides melt.

"*I was wrong . . .*" she said, more to herself than him. Then a sound of jubilation squeaked out her throat. She threw her arms around him, her soft body colliding against his, taking him off guard. With a grunt, he grabbed her waist and caught his balance just in time to keep them from tumbling down the stairs; his experienced hands instantly noted a delectable female shape.

"I'm so delighted it's you, Vincent," she said in his ear, seemingly unconcerned by their near fall. The soft scent of lavender emanated from her skin and tantalized his senses. She pulled away. "Come. I have something to show you." Grabbing hold of his hand, she raced up the stairs.

Accustomed to others ceding authority to him, Joseph found himself the one being led up the grand staircase. *Dieu, not your usual greeting.* A smile tugged at the corners of his mouth, amused by her antics despite himself. She was as delightfully unconventional in person as she was in her letters. This was, after all, "Vincent" and Emilie's first real meeting.

This was also Joseph and Emilie's first real meeting.

There hadn't been a real meeting ten years ago. Just a horrible fiasco.

Her warm hand securely holding his, she briskly walked ahead of him down the upstairs corridor, the shapeless cloak enveloping her form ruffling with each rapid step she took.

He shouldn't be here with her. He shouldn't have attended the Comtesse's masquerade because of her. Most assuredly, he should have ceased his letters long ago. And he was bent on believing it was nothing more than guilt that motivated the heightened attention he gave her.

Looking back every so often, she flashed him a smile. His groin tightened. This was the closest he'd been to her in a decade, and her mouth grabbed his focus each time she glanced his way. *Dieu.* There was no denying it. She had a pretty mouth. So lush. So perfect. The kind of mouth that could give a man hours of carnal pleasure.

Emilie reached her door and pulled him inside her private rooms.

It was late afternoon and the sun shone from the tall windows in the antechamber, giving the motifs adorning the walls of white and gold a warm glow.

"I'm so pleased you found me." She stopped in the middle of the antechamber, and released his hand. Oddly, he had the urge to grab hold of it again. "I've only just arrived and I was hoping I'd see you sooner rather than later. I'm glad I mentioned I'd be wearing a yellow cloak in my letter. Clearly it made it easy for you to find me."

Yellow cloak? He'd forgotten. He'd been too stunned by her plan to remember the details of her intended wardrobe.

With her usual smile on her distracting mouth, she pulled off her mask, tossing it onto a nearby settee, then her wig.

A mass of flaxen-colored curls tumbled out, looking so soft he wanted to reach out and play with a silky lock. Joseph drank in her visage. It was less girlish, more womanly now. Big fathomless green eyes. Hair as pale as moonlight. She was nothing short of ravishing.

With the face of an angel.

Taking hold of both his hands, she gave them an affectionate squeeze.

"Your turn," she said. "Remove your mask, Vincent."

His brows shot up in surprise. That sounded a lot like a command, not something he would have responded to favorably had someone else dared. But no one else but this unique woman would dare to make demands of any of Richard d'Alumbert, Duc de Vernant's sons. One of the most powerful men in the realm.

For the life of him, Joseph had no idea why he found her nonconforming ways so charming.

But he did. A lot.

Was this forwardness simply the way she was? Or perhaps she'd been secluded for so long that she wasn't accustomed to the usual rules of etiquette.

Joseph pulled off his mask, tossed it carelessly at the settee, and returned her smile.

Instantly, Emilie's smile dissolved. She took a step back.

Her reaction astonished him. "Emilie?"

Her smile returned. Not as bright. Nor as natural. "I'm sorry . . . it's just that . . ." She shook her head and waved off the rest of her sentence.

He frowned. "It's just *what?*" he pressed.

"It's nothing really. It's just . . . well, when you removed your mask, it felt as though I was staring at Joseph."

Merde.

"I know that's silly. You're identical . . ."

Not identical. Not in her eyes. In her eyes, Joseph was loathsome. He didn't know which bothered him more, that she despised him—when he'd never cared a whit what anyone thought.

Or that deep down inside, he couldn't fault her for the way she felt.

At some point during the last year he'd connected with her, when he'd normally maintained a comfortable level of detachment in all his dealings with women. This was yet another example of how far he'd let matters veer off course with this particular female.

Something he needed to rectify where she was concerned.

He was too uncomfortably aware of her. Too in tune with her emotions for his liking.

He wanted to snap the disconcerting connection.

"Actually, I'm far better looking than my brother," he jested, trying to leaven the moment and take the stricken look from her face.

Much to his delight, it worked. She burst into a laugh. A delicate sound he found appealing. "Well, now that we've established that, I have something I want you to see." She walked over to the writing desk.

He followed her, and tried to ignore her arousing scent.

"I asked my maid to unpack my books first," she said. "I wanted to show you a very special volume." Emilie leaned forward, searching through the books that were piled on the desk. Her cloak gaped open. Joseph got an instant view. Just above the décolletage of her gown he saw the top curves of her breasts. The sweetest most tempting tits. And even more surprising, the expanse of lovely—unmarred—skin.

Lavender-scented skin.

His cock stiffened. Joseph yanked his gaze to the stacks of books on the desk, in need of a distraction. He'd be damned if he was going to think about what else he'd find appealing under all those clothes. He'd thought about her body too many times, her scars be damned, especially on those nights when her innocent—yet so stirringly sensual—letters had him on fire. Asking him unabashed questions about sex. Confiding in him how and where she wanted to be touched. Taken.

There was no way he would allow her to torment him any more than she already was.

"Really. And what volume might that be?" he asked. A discussion about books was good. A neutral subject. One that wouldn't drive him to distraction.

"Ah, here it is." Picking up a book, she opened it and held up an illustration for him to see.

Before him was a graphic depiction of a naked woman bent over the edge of a bed while a man took her from behind.

Jésus-Christ.

"It's an erotic text," she announced.

No argument there. His eager prick gave a hungry throb in full agreement, as it now strained harder against the inside of his breeches.

She placed the book down on the desk, open to the inciting illustration. "I didn't realize there were so many positions to do this in." Her delicate brow furrowed. "I don't care for this one." She flipped a few pages forward. "I like pages five to twelve." Slowly she turned the pages, showing him her "favorites."

Heated illustration.

After heated illustration.

No doubt about it. Emilie would surely derive a measure of satisfaction if she knew the amount of torture she was presently inflicting on Joseph.

"Oh, and I like this one," she said, tapping the page. "This one" was a woman being taken while standing. Her back was against the wall as her lover drove his cock into her core. "Have you done this one, Vincent?"

All right. Enough was enough. Joseph closed the book, shutting out the stimulating images. The ones racing through his brain were another matter. He took a deep breath and let it out slowly.

"I'm not going to answer that." Thanks to his preoccupation with Emilie, he hadn't had sex in just over three months—if you added the days it took to arrive at the Comtesse's country estate and last night's baffling eve of abstinence. He was ready to climb out of his skin. The last thing he was going to do at the moment was engage in a sexual conversation with her. Not when images of Emilie's breasts and the damned depiction of the couple fucking against the wall were running rampant in his head. Only he was picturing taking this highly inquisitive virgin just the way she wanted. By God, he had the most powerful urge to sink his length into her, wondering just how tight her untried passage would be.

Her moss green eyes widened. "Oh? Why not? You've always answered my sexual questions before."

True. But that was through their correspondence. And not when she was standing in front of him looking like a sweet temptress, smelling better than any woman had a right to. His fingers itched to fist that silky blond hair, tilt her head back, and feast on that luscious mouth.

He was changing the subject.

"Why are you showing me this volume, Emilie?" There had to be a reason, other than to drive him mad.

Her smile returned to her comely face. "Because I know you have misgivings about my plans here. And as much as I appreciate your concern, I have the matter well in hand. As you can see, I've studied everything thoroughly. I am well prepared."

"Well prepared? You're contemplating having sex. Not going into battle, *ma belle*."

Emilie froze, his words unbalancing her.

Surely she hadn't heard correctly. Had he just called her . . . my *beauty*? No one had ever called her *that*. In fact, they'd called her just the opposite.

What could he possibly see that was beautiful?

There hadn't been a day in her life she'd felt pretty, much less beautiful . . . well, maybe just one time. One night. But it had turned from a dream to a nightmare.

You fool, he's simply being kind. Because that's what Vincent is. Kind. And he is— gracious God—pure male perfection . . .

Though she was trying, it was impossible to ignore his hard, chiseled body. His dark hair and knee-weakening blue eyes. Or the heat he inspired low in her belly. Vincent d'Alumbert was as disarming in person as he was in his letters.

His appeal wasn't tainted—like his brother Joseph's—by poor character.

And she was drawn to him. Intensely so.

He's waiting for a response, Emilie. Answer him . . . She cleared her throat and collected her wits. "I'm quite aware I'm not going into battle. I'm simply trying to assure you that I am fully knowledgeable about the subject of sex and seduction. Thanks to your answers as to what a man likes in bed, and my books, I am prepared to proceed."

He sighed. "Emilie—"

She silenced him by pressing a finger against his sensuous mouth. So warm and firm. Emilie tamped down the regret that surged inside her heart, knowing full well she'd never experience a kiss from this man. No man would knowingly indulge in an amorous encounter with *Charred and Scarred Emilie de Sarron*. The only way for her to have some pleasure of her own was to be with a man who didn't know her. Didn't know she'd been marred in a fire. "I know what you're going to say. One needs to experience sex to be truly knowledgeable." Reluctantly, she removed her finger. She liked touching him. A little too much for her own good. "I agree wholeheartedly. That is why I'm going to have my first experience tonight."

He scrubbed a hand down his face. "Emilie, there is nothing wrong with anonymous sex. People do it all the time. But a man is going to want . . . " Vincent faltered.

"To have me naked," she supplied.

"Exactly. It's part of the pleasure. Skin against skin. Sex involves the senses, touch, taste, smell, sight. A man is going to want to see—"

"I'll manage." The words came out sharper than she'd intended. She didn't want to be abrupt, but his comments were undermining her confidence. And being in the presence of this sinfully gorgeous Aristo—whose letters oozed charm and had made her laugh, who'd impressed her with his intellect and candidness, and who'd given her the most tantalizing insight into a man's mind during sex—made it difficult to concentrate on her plan.

The allure of Vincent d'Alumbert was even stronger in person than she'd imagined. And she had to resist it. It was bad enough her feelings for him ran deeper than she'd like. She wasn't going to dwell on what she couldn't have in her life—a man of her own.

This delicious man.

Why long for something that was impossible? Instead, she was going to focus on what she could have.

And she could have some bliss in her life.

Nothing was going to stop her.

"You are a dear friend, Vincent," she said. "You've done a great deal for me already and . . . I loathe to ask for a favor. Or rather two favors . . ."

His eyes narrowed slightly. "What two favors?"

"I know you want me to succeed. But if I'm to concentrate on finding the right man to give myself too, I need you to keep Joseph away."

He stiffened slightly. *"And . . . ?"*

She smiled. "Oh, and I need you to help me choose a lover."

CHAPTER THREE

Merde! He must be mad, utterly insane, to have come here and made himself a party to this!

Joseph stalked down the corridor on his way to the grand dining hall. The "favors" she'd requested had echoed in his head since he left her. Hours later, his ire was full blown. White-hot. Prickling his skin.

. . . help me choose a lover. The hell he would! He didn't care how troubled his conscience was. He would not do her bidding. He didn't do anyone's bidding.

And he certainly did *not* find women their bed sport.

Dieu! She'd actually asked for his help in finding someone to bed her.

He could only imagine the amusement his brothers would derive from learning a woman had made that request of him.

Chatter and laughter emanated from the dining hall, violin music drifting through the din. Joseph secured his demi-mask in place just before he reached the threshold.

I need you to keep Joseph away . . .

Oh, he was going to stay away, all right. No problem there.

Once and for all he was going to stop voicing his concerns. In fact, he wasn't going to be concerned. He wasn't going to think about her attempts to be debauched tonight. Or worry about how disastrously it might turn out.

For his involvement ten years ago, he owed her an apology— one he couldn't even offer because she wanted nothing to do with Joseph—but that was *all*. He didn't owe her a *lover*.

He wasn't getting involved with this plan of hers. No matter what.

She was a grown woman. She'd made her decision.

And he was making his: He'd decided Emilie de Sarron had occupied his thoughts long enough. She wasn't going to be a mental distraction anymore. Or a physical one. While she gave herself to God knows who and attempted God knows which sex act she'd chosen from her book, Joseph was going to do what he should have been doing at the Comtesse's masquerade from the start.

Delving into some much needed sexual oblivion.

Joseph entered the grand dining hall. The mirrors on the walls reflected the candlelight from the wall sconces and the four large silver candelabras on the long linen-covered dining table that ran down the center of the room. Guests were more boisterous than the usual noble gathering. No formalities or respectable social conduct on display here. Not when the purpose of the evening meal was to find a partner or partners for carnal entertainment afterward.

Open fondling and flirting were everywhere.

Joseph marched straight to his usual seat near the head of the table. His brothers and his friend, Georges, Marquis d'Attel, occupied the chairs near him.

"There you are. I was beginning to wonder if you were going to show up," Vincent said with a smile. "We still don't know where you disappeared to last night."

Into a brandy decanter. Fool that he was.

Joseph snatched the crystal goblet off the table and held it up. A servant was quick to appear and fill the vessel with wine. He downed it, and held it up again for more, eager to take the edge off his vexation. The sooner his irritation subsided, the sooner he could begin to enjoy himself. It surprised even him just how furious he was. And he refused to dwell on or attempt to decipher why her requests had made him *this* incensed. "I've been occupied. And last night is none of your concern."

Georges laughed. "Now that's evasive."

Seated on the other side of Vincent, Gilbert leaned toward Joseph, grinning from behind his gilded demi-mask. "An answer that begs the question: Just who were you 'occupied' with?" He elbowed Vincent. "Wouldn't you say, Vincent?"

Vincent was sporting the same foolish grin. "I would."

"In case it's escaped your notice, we are at a masquerade," Joseph stated sharply. "You're not supposed to know whom you're with." For his mental peace, he wished he didn't know Emilie was here. And he didn't want to know whom she'd be with tonight.

"Ah, my fine friends." Henri de Villeneuve strolled up and placed a hand on Joseph's shoulder. "Did any of you happen to notice our friend, Augustin de Coix?" Smiling, Henri gestured down the table with a motion of his chin. "He's actually found a woman who can tolerate him. She looks new."

That grabbed Joseph's attention. He shot his gaze down the table, spotting his friend Augustin, Comte de Coix, immediately. And the woman he was with. She was wearing a blue and gold demi-mask, dressed in a light blue cloak. His stomach plummeted.

Emilie.

His arm resting on the back of her chair, Augustin leaned into her, his mouth at her ear as he whispered to her, relaying an intimate message. Joseph's body went rigid.

"I don't believe I've ever seen her before," Henri said. "Have you?"

"Isn't that the woman who arrived this afternoon?" Vincent asked.

"No." Joseph mentally winced. The denial shot out of his mouth a little too abruptly.

Merde. Of all the men in the room, she'd picked Augustin? He was a self-proclaimed ass. He wouldn't satisfy her. He'd no skill or finesse in bed. Nor did he care to. He'd take his pleasure, then take his leave.

He was all wrong for her purposes. Damn it, he was wrong for her. Period.

Emilie smoothed a hand down the front of her cloak, bringing attention to it. *Dieu*, she was the only one wearing one. Of all the different costumes worn by the women in the room, from moderate to outrageous, Emilie's cloak stood out. It all but screamed, "Emilie de Sarron." How much longer before his friends realized it was her?

"Look at the way she's dressed." The comment came from Gilbert's mouth, making Joseph want to throttle his youngest brother.

"I like the way she's dressed," Georges said.

"Hmmm, me, too," Henri concurred.

Joseph shot them a look, one that must have indicated just how stunned he was by their response.

Henri's brows shot up. "What? You don't agree? Look at her, Joseph. She's a comely little piece." A slow smile spread across his mouth. "When the ladies present are wearing low-cut décolletages, our clever little seductress wears a cloak, just to make her stand out."

"Absolutely," Vincent concurred. "She's made it a game. Just think of the fun it will be to peel away those layers and sample the tasty fruit within."

"She is clever," Georges said. "She's donned the cloak just to tantalize our imagination. Every man who looks at her is forced to wonder at the delicious form she's hidden under it."

Good Lord. Not at all the reaction he'd imagined.

Just then Augustin reached and yanked open Emilie's cloak. She started and, with a charming smile, gently closed the cloak again, rose, and left her seat. With nothing but elegance and grace.

Laughter burst out of Joseph's brothers and two friends.

"It doesn't look as though the lady is impressed with our Augustin," Henri said, still chuckling.

Joseph couldn't shake the sense of relief he felt as he watched her walk away from Augustin. Nor could he help but marvel at the way she'd handled herself. Despite her lack of experience, she hadn't let Augustin's brutish advances rattle her.

It occurred to him just then that her chances of succeeding with her plan were great. Aside from her intellect, she was even braver than he'd given her credit for.

Emilie wasn't going to be frightened away, like some faint-hearted ingénue.

One man in this room was going to be the first to enjoy this most exceptional woman. A woman who happened to have the sweetest face, and the softest green eyes he'd ever seen.

A foreign emotion hit him in the gut.

Joseph battled it back.

Just then he felt feminine fingers brush across his cheek. Looking up, he found an attractive dark-haired woman standing beside his chair, smiling down at him. Sporting a bright green demi-mask that matched the color of her gown, she wore a décolletage that was so very low, he wondered if she would spill out at any moment.

"Good evening, my handsome lord," she all but purred. "I fear I have a dilemma. I wondered if you might assist me?"

"Oh? What is your dilemma?" he asked.

Her smile turned saucy as she twirled a lock of her hair around her finger. "It seems that all the seats are taken. I haven't anywhere to sit. I don't suppose you'd allow me to use your lap?"

He heard muted snickers from the fools he associated with.

"I never turn away a lady in distress." Taking her hand, Joseph pulled her down onto his lap. "Allow me to be of assistance."

"Why, thank you, kind sir." She snuggled against his groin, her ample bosom looking even more plentiful from his new vantage point. Right under his face.

She slipped an arm around his shoulders and brought them closer to him. "You may call me Julie." A false name. Everyone used them. He loved the anonymity of it all.

She brought her mouth near his ear. "I am in your debt. I am all yours, my lord . . ." And began nibbling down his neck. Light little bites.

Now *this* was exactly what he should be focusing on. A sexual encounter with someone he didn't know. Someone who would never cross his mind afterward.

Joseph closed his eyes, eager to lose himself in the sensations, but the moment they were shut, words Emilie had written rushed into his mind.

I want to know what it feels like to have a man inside me. To know the sensations of each plunge and drag as he takes me to the ultimate fulfillment. Oh, I long to know firsthand how glorious is it to be in a lover's embrace, lost in passion, locked in the most intimate joining . . .

Joseph's eyes flew open. He cursed the mental diversion. *Don't think about her. Not now. Focus on the woman at hand.* He wasn't going to think about Emilie. Or if the man she chose would give her the pleasure she sought and deserved.

Julie placed a hand on his chest, and slowly inched her way lower and lower.

"A bet, gentlemen," he heard Georges say. "A hundred *louis d'or* says I fuck the lovely lady with the cloak first."

"A hundred *louis d'or* says you fail and I succeed," Henri challenged.

Joseph arrested Julie's hand and forgot all about the woman on his lap.

Her head shot up. "My lord?"

He ignored her, because the next thing he heard was Gilbert announce, "I'll bet, too." Gilbert drained his goblet, his smile returning the moment he set the vessel back down on the table. "You gentlemen don't stand a chance when pitted against my charm."

Georges and Henri scoffed as they rose from their chairs.

"I go first," Georges said.

Fuck. Despite the woman in his arms, Joseph was on his feet in an instant, and handed Julie off to Georges. Georges grunted when she landed in his arms.

"There will be no bet!" Joseph decreed, accustomed to ruling his friends. "No one is having her." Words shot out of his mouth, without censor.

His friends and brothers exchanged curious glances. Joseph knew he sounded like a lunatic. Given the type of gathering they were at, he could hardly make such a statement. But he didn't care. Emilie was sexually untried. His corrupt friends wouldn't be gentle with her. Or take her with care, even if they knew it was her first time.

And the mere thought of them recognizing her in the throes of passion and saying something cruel to her tore at his very vitals.

He wasn't going to let them hurt her again, like he'd let them hurt her ten years ago.

"I'm having her," he added for good measure. "Go find someone else to amuse you."

Georges put Julie down. "Ah, come now. You can't claim exclusivity here. We can all share her."

Joseph narrowed his eyes. "I'll claim whatever I want. Find. Someone. Else." He looked pointedly at each man before him.

That prompted Julie to turn on a heel, miffed, and stalk away.

"Gentlemen, I'd like a private word with Joseph." Vincent, who'd been silent until now, finally spoke up. The others walked away, grumbling.

"Brother, you lead and they follow. And for the most part, I don't mind going along, but"—he crossed his arms—"you don't dictate whom I bed. Now then, care to tell me who this woman is?"

"She's wearing a mask. How the hell should I know who she is?" He hated lying to Vincent, but the truth was far more complicated than his deceit. And more difficult to explain. There were things about what was going on that he couldn't explain to himself. And didn't want to try.

His twin sighed and shook his head. "Fine. Have it your way. You don't know her. She's got you intrigued, or some such nonsense. I'm still having her," Vincent said with finality.

Joseph's gut tightened. "Not until I'm done with her," was all he could respond. Pressing the matter any further would make him sound as though he'd gone completely mad. As it was, his behavior was absurd, bordering on irrational. He'd never cared who a woman was with before, during, or after he'd had her.

Vincent silently contemplated his words. Joseph's heart pounded away the seconds, wondering what he'd have to do to keep Vincent away if he didn't agree.

His brother's genial smile returned. "Agreed. You have her first. She's all yours tonight." He patted him on the back. "I get her tomorrow."

*****

Their bodies touched.

He drew his arm around Emilie's waist and pulled her up tightly against him. Then he pressed his lips to hers. It was actually happening. Her first real kiss. An amorous encounter of her very own. His tongue snaked into her mouth and was presently swirling about. It felt, well . . . odd. But then she'd no experience in this area, and her masked gentleman was seemingly enjoying himself if the zealous sounds he emitted were any indication.

Emilie relaxed her shoulders and laced her arms around his neck, throwing herself eagerly into the kiss, anxiously waiting for the moment "it" would hit her. Passion. Hunger.

That all-consuming desire.

Just like the couple she saw in the corridor earlier. Just like the books she'd devoured again and again. *Just like you felt near Vincent . . .*

She'd purposely led her masked lover to the gardens. The perfect setting. They were under an indigo sky with a large luminescent moon and a thousand twinkling stars. What could be more perfect? All she had to do was let her lover take the lead, ignore the grunts from the couple who were mostly naked, rutting in the distance. And of course, resist the urge to pretend the man kissing her was Vincent d'Alumbert.

Just focus. Any moment now, she'd be swept up in "it."

Mimicking his tongue swirls, she angled her head farther to the right and hoped she was doing this correctly. He seemed to like it. He'd pulled her against him tighter, and groaned louder.

Minutes later, he was squeezing her right breast through her cloak and "it" was still nowhere to be found.

Worse, she was actually . . . bored.

This experience was of the blandest sort.

What was she doing wrong? He was handsome, or at least he appeared to be from what she could see of his face that wasn't covered with his demi-mask. There was nothing unpleasant about him. Not his smell or his taste. What was amiss here? Where was the heat? The exhilaration?

"Ah, there you are," Emilie heard just before a strong arm slid in between her and the man kissing her, and pulled her back, breaking their contact.

She jerked her head up and was surprised to find herself staring at Vincent, his arm still across her chest, holding her shoulder. He wore his mask, and the same attire he had on earlier. She knew it was him. He gripped her elbow. "Come with me."

"Just a moment, monsieur! Where do you think you're going with her?" her flavorless lover protested.

Vincent turned back around and shoved his mask off his face, a scowl etched across his handsome features.

"Oh, it's you, Valle . . . *Joseph* . . ." The gentleman's anger was immediately mollified.

"It's Vincent, you fool. The lady is coming with me. Any objections?" The question was weighty with authority, his elevated rank hanging in the air between the men. It was clear what was truly being asked: "Do you *dare* object?"

Her anonymous kisser glanced at her, his expression looking remarkably like regret and then said a soft, "No."

With that, Vincent took her hand and stalked toward the château with her in tow, the tiny stones on the path crunching beneath her feet.

She was all but running to keep up, her free hand holding her cloak closed so it wouldn't fly open.

His comportment irked her. "Vincent, just what do you think you're doing?"

He didn't respond and kept on walking.

"Vincent, you just bullied that man." It bothered her to see it. He'd swooped in, without excuses or apologies. A display that was more in keeping with Joseph's character and not the Vincent she'd come to know. "Your conduct was rather poor, don't you think?"

Still no answer. Her ire spiked. She'd no idea what had gotten into him.

"Just because you're the son of the Duc de Vernant doesn't mean you're above reproach."

"You're wrong there. I'm afraid it does." His answer annoyed her further, as did the fact that he was affecting her. The simple touch of his hand was sending tiny tingles reverberating up her arm to her breasts. Hardening her nipples. She'd spend long minutes kissing her masked gentleman with no reaction. Not a spark of heat. Yet some simple handholding with this man, and her body was aquiver.

It was exasperating. Vincent was a friend, albeit an annoying one at the moment. She didn't delude herself into believing he'd ever desire her. "I don't care a whit who your father is, you're not above reproach with me."

"Believe me, I'm very much aware of that."

His response surprised her. "Vincent, where are we going? What is all this about? I was in the middle of an amorous encounter when you so rudely interrupted." All right, perhaps she was a tad grateful that he'd put an end to the dull experience, but he didn't need to know that. What he needed to know was that she wouldn't tolerate any high-handedness from him.

"You were in the middle of an encounter, *chère*. It was hardly amorous. You looked ready to fall asleep. Trust me, I did you a favor."

Before she could offer up a hot retort, they entered the château's great room. There was a crush of people now. People who'd clearly consumed more drink, the laughter louder and the throng rowdier than before. Bawdy behavior was more evident and widespread. The light fondling she'd seen earlier around the table had been replaced by open groping. There were more than a few open bodices. Bare breasts. Open breeches. And in a few instances, open coupling.

Emilie was dragged past a giggling woman sitting on her lover's lap. Her masked man nibbled at the grapes nestled between her amble breasts, making her squirm and squeal with delight. Vincent continued through the crowd, maneuvering her out of the Grand Salon, through the grand vestibule, up the staircase, and down the corridor straight to her private rooms.

When she was finally standing in her antechamber, she pulled off her mask and wig and demanded, "Tell me what we're doing here."

"You're leaving. Now. This night." He tore off his mask and tossed it carelessly to the floor. "Where are your trunks?" Vincent turned and marched into her bedchambers.

She chased him in. "What do you mean, I'm leaving tonight? Why on earth would I do that?"

"I'll get someone to help you pack. Better yet, I'll help." He strode to the armoire and threw open the doors. "*Dieu*, you have a lot of clothes . . . Are there more in the cabinet?"

He, a d'Alumbert, privileged and pampered, was going to help her pack? Tackle the task of a *servant*?

"Vincent, what has gotten into you? Have you lost your mind?"

"I've ask myself that question many times since your recent arrival." He raked a hand though his dark hair. "Emilie, you can't stay. You must leave. The sooner the better."

She frowned. "Why?"

"Because this plan of yours isn't going to work."

"Really?" Emilie tilted her head to one side. "And why not?"

Joseph noted the stubborn look in her eyes. One that told him she wasn't about to leave without a good reason. *Think of one.*

"Fine. You force me to tell you," he said.

"Tell me what?"

"Joseph wants you." That wasn't a lie. Though he wished it was. "I can't keep him away." That wasn't a lie either. He couldn't seem to stay away from her no matter how he tried. And he couldn't keep Vincent away from her either.

His easy-mannered twin, who'd always done as Joseph asked, picked a fine time to be unyielding.

Her lips twitched as though she were holding back a smile. "That's it? That is the reason I must flee in the middle of the night?" She approached, the smile on her beautiful face growing larger with each step she took. "That's why you interrupted me in such haste?" She stopped before him. Lavender swirled around him, stirring his senses.

His blood warmed. "Ah . . . yes."

She gave him a radiant smile. "Vincent, you're a dear!" She threw herself against him, her arms entwining his neck.

Desire hit him in a hot wave on contact. His cock thickened as he took in the warm press of her body down the length of his and her silky flaxen hair against his cheek.

"I'm so moved by your concern. You're a wonderful, wonderful friend." She tightened her arms around him and snuggled in closer, inadvertently rubbing his engorged prick with her belly. *Dieu . . .*

He didn't deserve the praise and he certainly couldn't take the physical contact, given his current celibate state.

Gently, Joseph pushed her away. Placing his hands on her shoulders, he held her at arm's length and dipped his head, bringing him eyelevel to her. Big beautiful green eyes started back at him, drawing him in. Just as distracting was that perfect pink mouth. Seeing another man sampling her drove him half insane. He was starved for that mouth. Ludicrous as it was, he wanted it all to himself when he'd never cared much about exclusivity before. Thoughts of sliding his cock between those lush lips flitted through his mind. "So you see now why you must leave," he forced out, ignoring the mental images. "It's quite impossible to keep Joseph from you. He's told me he'll approach you tomorrow. And we both know how much you don't want that. Correct?"

"Correct."

"Wonderful. Then it's settled. You're leaving. Let's pack." Joseph released her shoulders and walked toward the cabinet where he was sure to find more of her wardrobe, then thought better of it. He'd no idea how to pack. And no interest in learning. Joseph turned back around to face her. "Better yet, I'll go see to your carriage and I'll have your personal effects packed and sent to you." Resting his hands on his hips, he smiled, feeling at ease for the first time since he'd arrived at the Comtesse's château, despite his stiff prick.

"I'm not leaving."

His smile died. As did his easy feeling.

"What do you mean, you're not leaving?" That stubborn look was back, her expression serious and uncompromising.

"I may not want Joseph to approach me. But I won't leave because of him."

Merde. "Emilie, we're talking about *Joseph*. Remember, horrible, terrible Joseph? You don't want him anywhere near you. You've said so. It's best you leave."

"Actually, since you put it that way, I've changed my mind."

His smile returned. "Excellent!"

"I want Joseph to approach me."

His smiled died again. *Jésus-Christ.* There had to be something wrong with his hearing. "You *want* Joseph to approach you?" he repeated, incredulous.

"I do. In fact, I welcome his advances. I'll even encourage them. Then I'll do something he deserves. I'll rebuff him. He has it coming, don't you think?"

Joseph blinked. Speechless. Emilie de Sarron was torturing him.

On every level imaginable.

She smiled. "Heir to the Duc de Vernant, the mighty Joseph d'Alumbert, Marquis de Valle, contemptible and vile, whom society bends to, and placates at every turn . . . He has never been refused anything. Nor has he ever had a woman turn him down. I think I'll enjoy doing just that—refusing him. Turning him away."

Joseph rubbed his forehead, trying to knead away the dull ache that had just developed. Yet the discomfort was small in comparison to his throbbing cock. He couldn't believe it, but he was hard for a woman who'd just called him contemptible and vile. To his face.

Having mastered the art of seduction long ago, he'd fucked his way through the French court, and yet this one sexual novice had utterly seduced him—with the strokes of her quill, no less. A woman who didn't dress provocatively and had injuries to her body. And nothing—absolutely nothing—seemed to diminish his desire for her. His fever continued to mount to the point where it was influencing his behavior. His actions idiotic. Because no matter how hard he tried to ignore it or silence it, his every rakish instinct told him that a sexual experience with this unique woman would be nothing short of pure ecstasy. Clearly some otherworld forces were at play. How else could he explain being so ridiculously spellbound? Someone somewhere was making certain he was going to pay for all his misdeeds. Every one of them. This night. At the hand of this woman.

What poetic justice.

He took a deep breath and let it out slowly. "Emilie, don't toy with Joseph, or any man here. No man likes a cock tease. By your attendance at the masquerade, it is assumed you are willing to be taken. Playing the coquette here, with no intention of surrendering sexually, is most unwise. With anyone."

"Rape isn't permitted, if that's what you're suggesting," she countered.

"What I'm suggesting is that a man may not think you are seriously objecting if you lead him down the path too far. In a setting such as this, people play a variety of sex games and roles."

She was silent, and he could tell she was carefully considering his words. "I won't seek out Joseph, but if he approaches me, he will be played upon, and in the end, if he refuses to take no for an answer, he will be cast out of the masquerade. This is, after all, my aunt's home."

Joseph wanted to tell her that her aunt would never—could never—shut her doors to any member of the house of Alumbert, but he kept silent.

"As for the other men here, I don't intend to withhold myself. I want to surrender sexually, as long as they are not Joseph's friends. You don't understand, Vincent. I need this. I want a lover. I want to touch and be touched. To know the physical bliss that you and others have known."

"What if in the throes of passion, he tries to remove all your clothing?"

She tensed. An emotion he couldn't decipher crossed her features. Damn it. The words had tumbled from his mouth. He hadn't meant to voice them, but the gnawing fear wouldn't relent.

"That isn't your concern," she responded tightly. "I'm staying. I'm proceeding as planned and that is final."

She turned on her heel, picked up her mask and wig, and headed for the door.

Joseph held back the profanities he wanted to bellow out of sheer frustration. Between his brother, Emilie, and this disastrous situation he'd created, he was sure to lose his mind.

Emilie was heading back out there, looking for a lover. Not a single man here deserved her. Least of all him. Joseph was the last person she'd want to touch her. To take her innocence. But when she placed a hand on the door handle, he shouted:

"I'll be your lover."

Her hand on the door handle, Emilie stared back at him. She didn't move. Nor say a word. Her sweet lips slightly parted, she looked frozen in shock.

He shouldn't have said he'd bed her. But he wouldn't take it back. There were numerous reasons why having her was wrong. And just as many reasons why this felt so right.

Maybe if he showed her just how desirable she really was, it would make amends for his transgressions against her. He hated it that she'd hidden herself away for years. That she hid inside all those layers of clothes. And most especially that she believed she couldn't stir a man's blood unless she masked that angelic face and her identity.

He wanted to prove her wrong.

By no means was he being selfless here. Selfishly, he wanted to be the one to touch her and be touched by her. To take this passionate, headstrong—untaught—female and initiate her into the sexual pleasures she so adamantly wanted to experience. By God, he wanted to fuck her so badly, it made his body ache and the crest of his cock wet with pre-come.

As it was, his sac was drawn up painfully tight. He was ready to explode.

He was going to have her. Tonight. Now. And satisfy both their needs.

And once he did, this incessant carnal craving for her, this vexing captivation would end. No?

CHAPTER FOUR

He jests, Emilie told herself, her heart pounding hard. Scrutinizing his face, she looked for any sign that would confirm it.

His sensuous blue eyes gazed back at her, unflinching. Try as she might, she couldn't find any insincerity in his expression. Nothing that belied his words.

Dear God, he actually looked *serious*. He couldn't be. Why would he be?

"Why . . . ?" The word rushed out of her lungs on a breath, unable to muster more.

His brow furrowed. "Why what, *chère?*"

"Why would you want to be *my* lover?" The man could have any woman he wanted. With prominence, power, and fine looks, the d'Alumbert brothers were never short on female attention. They had their choice of mistresses. All of whom were beautiful and flawless.

She was neither.

The corner of his mouth lifted with a slight smile. He approached, all male grace and masculine beauty, and stopped before her. Her heart thundered so hard now, he was certain to hear it.

Vincent took her hand and, to her utter astonishment, lifted it to his mouth and pressed his lips to the sensitive spot on the inside of her wrist. A thrill shot up her arm. She felt a quickening in her belly.

He brought her hand to the bulge in his breeches and stroked her palm over his thick length. So large and solid. A feral need throbbed through her core and weakened her knees. "This is what you do to me, Emilie. You stiffen my cock anytime I'm near you. Anytime I think of you. Anytime I read one of your letters where you tell me, bold as can be, your sexual fantasies. *I want you.*"

She was trembling all over, when she'd never trembled for anyone. This couldn't be real. It had to be a dream. One she'd had of him more times than she'd care to count.

He leaned in, his lips grazing across her cheek to stop at her ear. "There isn't a man here who knows you better than I do. I know what you want. How you want it. I can satisfy all your desires." Her breaths were ragged. Her head was spinning and her knees almost gave out when he whispered, "I'll take you in every one of your favorite positions—pages five to twelve of your erotic book. Then I'll take you in some of my favorite ways. You'll enjoy every moment. All you have to do is say yes, *ma belle.*"

At his endearment, she jumped back, bumping against the wall. *My beauty* . . . Tears welled in her eyes. She blinked them back, embarrassed by them. She didn't allow herself to cry. Not for years. And never in front of others.

She reeled, trying to make sense of it all.

My beauty . . . It was the second time he'd said it, and with the same level of sincerity. How could he mean it?

"You . . . You want . . . *me?*" It seemed too incredible to conceive, despite the physical proof of his desire.

His half smile returned. "We both do."

"Both?"

"My prick and I." He crossed his arms, his smile broadening. "We are in complete accord on the matter. We both want me to bed you."

Oh God. Beautiful Vincent d'Alumbert desired *her.*

No man had ever desired her. Or ever would. Or so she'd come to believe after years of mean-spirited commentary and a night of abject humiliation where future suitors had indicated their scorn.

He took a step toward her. "Emilie . . ."

"I don't understand . . . You say you want me . . . but you know I have s—"

"Such a beautiful face?" he injected. "I know. You're rather breathtaking."

Breathtaking? She shook her head. "That's not what I was going to say. I have bur—"

"Breasts." He pressed his palms against the wall on either side of her head, hemming her in. "Very nice breasts, actually. I got a glimpse of them when your cloak opened."

He did? Nice breasts? "No . . . That's not it at all. What I'm trying to say . . . I have . . ." She forced the bitter words off her tongue. *"Burns.* And scars. I have scars and burns." At the moment, she hated them more than ever.

He leaned in, his mouth so close to her own, making her lips warm and tingle. "I'm still hard for you. I still want you."

Fresh unshed tears blurred her sight.

Gracious God. If this was a dream, she didn't want to wake up.

"What—What about our friendship, Vincent? I don't want to lose that . . ." She didn't have many dear friends. And none like him.

"A few days and nights of carnal diversions won't change anything. It's only while we're here. You've come to find a man to show you sexual pleasure. Let me be that man." He brushed his lips ever so lightly against hers. Her nerve endings quivered with life. She parted her lips for him, but he pulled away. "You won't be bored with me," he wickedly promised. "And you don't need to wear a mask with me either." He tugged it and the wig from her grip and dropped them to the floor.

"Let me give you what you want." Vincent slipped his hand inside her cloak and cupped her breast. She sucked in a breath. His thumb began drawing scintillating circles around her nipple. Each circular caress making her feel weak and wet. Her sex, slick and needy. The hardened tip of her breast was straining for him, aching for his touch. "I'll make you come . . .hard . . . again and again." He grazed his thumb over her sensitized nipple, tearing a soft cry from her. "All you have to do is surrender to me. Say, ye—"

She shot up onto the balls of her feet, fisted his justacorps, and crushed her mouth against his.

Vincent pushed her up against the wall firmly. Cupping her face, he took command of the kiss, tilting her head to the side, sliding his tongue past her lips, possessing her mouth in a delicious, unhurried kiss. Unlike her masked lover in the gardens, Vincent gave her slow, luscious strokes with his tongue, sending waves of pleasure rippling through her. The bud between her legs began to pulse. He kissed even better than she'd imagined any man could. Emilie tightened her grip on his coat, a moan escaping her throat.

Her breaths erratic, she kissed him with urgency, unable to hold to his languorous pace. His taste was intoxicating. She couldn't get enough, sucking and stroking his tongue with famished zeal. This was "it." The hunger and heat she sought. Her fever mounted by the moment.

Then his lips were gone. Her eyes flew open. Dazed and bereft, she stared back at him, unable to catch her breath.

He was smiling. "I just knew you were going to taste that good. And be that passionate. I can't wait to taste the rest of you. I'm going to savor every sweet drop."

His comment made her insides quiver. "That's odd . . . I was going to say the same thing."

His brows lifted, then he burst into a laugh. He pushed her back against the wall and gave her a fast fierce kiss she felt all the way down to her toes.

"I can't wait to have you, spirited and sensual Emilie de Sarron," he murmured, his mouth on the sensitive spot below her ear, slowly moving down her neck.

Emilie closed her eyes.

Oh my . . . No one had ever called her *that*. His words coiled around her heart. She cautioned herself. It would be too easy to fall wildly in love with him. And she couldn't.

This was only an affair. Of the temporary variety.

This is going to happen. Vincent is going to be your lover . . . She'd be pleasured by this beautiful Aristo, reputed for his carnal skills. His sexual talents matched only by his twin. Better still, her first amorous encounter would be with a man who actually mattered to her.

And she was seizing the opportunity with eager hands.

Joseph slipped his arm around her waist and pulled her up against him, crushing his cock against her belly. Relishing the feel of her against his body. His prick gave a hungry throb. He'd never taken a virgin. Never found the notion of having an inexperienced woman in bed enticing. Yet he wanted to sink his length inside this woman more than he wanted his next breath.

Grasping the fabric of her cloak with one hand, Joseph pulled it open, unveiling her. She stiffened and tried to pull away. He tightened his arm around her waist. "Easy. You're safe with me." He moved his gaze down her slender neck to the swells of her breasts above her décolletage. Luscious mounds rose and fell with her quickened breaths. The expanse of satiny skin beckoned and beguiled him. Lightly, he ran his fingertips over the curves of her breasts along the scooped neckline. She jerked in his arms. He could feel her racing heart. He could see her nipples were hard and pressing against the inside of her gown. And he could only imagine how sweet those little tips would taste on his tongue. When he met her gaze, he found her eyes were darker with passion. "The cloak has to go." He kept his voice soft but firm.

"My cloak?" There was a touch of alarm in her tone.

"We'll remove as much of your clothing as you're comfortable with, but the cloak goes." He wasn't going to relent on this. "You have a gown on. You don't need it, and quite frankly, I hate it."

"Really?" She looked down at the thing. "I thought it was pretty."

Dieu, she'd worn them for so long, she actually did. No matter what color or expensive fabrics she chose, it was no more than a shapeless mantle that hung from shoulder to ankle. A different way to hide herself from society. He wasn't going to let her. He didn't want to see her hidden behind it any longer. She should never have been made to feel she needed to conceal herself in the first place. He was determined to coax her clothing off her layer by layer. By the end of the week, she was going to be naked in his bed. Not for a moment did he believe she could repel him, no matter what her scars looked like.

And he had a strong suspicion he knew exactly where on her body they were located. In every illustration she favored in her erotic volume the woman faced her lover. The marring had to be on her back. Something to keep in mind as he disrobed her.

"Sex is about mutual pleasure, and it pleases me to see more of you. Take it off, Emilie." He dipped his head and lightly bit her soft earlobe. He liked her little gasp. "Do it. I'll make it worth your while."

Reluctantly, he released her and stepped back. Like a curtain, the cloak closed again, cocooning her within. He waited. Impatiently. Fighting back the urge to rip the thing off for her.

A myriad of emotions crossed her face. She vacillated. *Merde.* Seeing her struggle with the removal of a simple cloak pierced him to the core—proof just how greatly the teasing and taunts she'd endured had affected her. Yet for all they'd put her through, incredibly she hadn't become caustic or bitter. As many would have in her place. She was quick to smile. Sweet and affectionate. Passionate, provocative and intelligent. Engaging in every way.

She hadn't allowed anyone to break her true spirit.

She amazed him. He admired her. Something he couldn't say about most of the people he knew.

Silently he willed her to discard the cloak. Wanting it more for her than for himself.

Slowly she raised her hands and grasped the fastenings. His heart soared. Averting her gaze, she loosened the ties, and pulled the cloak off her shoulders. It fell to the floor.

She wore a light blue gown trimmed with yellow ribbons, and it accentuated her delectable feminine attributes—her body clearly defined before him for the first time. His mouth went dry. Even though he knew she had a luscious form, he was unprepared for the vision she'd be without the cloak.

"*Jésus-Christ*, you're ravishing," he breathed. By her expression, it was obvious his comment had unbalanced her. He'd noted the same reaction each time he complimented her. He was bloody well going to keep giving them until she believed him.

"Come here, Emilie." He suddenly felt angry. All this loveliness senselessly shrouded. For years. He was going to make it up to her. In every way he could. Starting with giving her the sexual pleasure she sought and making her come harder than she'd ever imagined.

She stepped closer, her slight frown telling him she didn't care for the sharpness of his tone.

He captured her chin. "From now on, whenever we're alone, you'll not wear that cloak. Or any cloak. Do you understand?" She opened her mouth to respond, but he continued. "You'll not wear any caleçons for the rest of the week either."

"Not wear my cloak or my drawers?" Disbelief was in her voice.

He placed his hands on her shoulders and pressed her back against the wall. "That's correct. In fact, *ma belle*, it's an order. Your sweet little sex is all mine for the next few days. You're going to give me easy access to it, and I'll have you frequently and anytime I want." He smiled. "I catch you wearing either, I may just have to punish you in whatever wicked method I choose."

Curiosity flared in her green eyes. He loved it that his words didn't put her off. Instead they spiked her interest. Seeing it sent a shot of hot excitement through his body, causing his cock to seep more spunk. He had to have her. Soon. After months of mounting desire for her, he couldn't take much more.

She tilted her head to one side, those magnificent eyes studying him. "I'm seeing a rather overbearing side of you tonight. For your information, I don't respond to orders." The mischief in her expression belied her stern tone. "I am, however, open to bargaining."

"Bargaining?"

"Yes, I'll cede if . . ."

"If?"

"You kiss me again." She was doing a poor job of hiding her smile.

He felt a smile tugging at his own mouth. Her response was novel, yet typical for Emilie, who did everything outside the norm. So unlike the women he cavorted with, who leaped at his commands in the boudoir, eager to remain in his favor. Emilie bargained. What she didn't know was just how much power she could wield. Truth be told, she had considerable leverage to bargain with. He'd agree to just about anything to have her.

"A kiss," he said. "That's all it's going to take, is it?"

"For now," was her saucy response.

Dieu, how he wanted to fuck her.

"Very well. Agreed," he said. "Open the front of your gown." Her smile died. *"Pardon . . . ?"*

"You didn't say where you wanted to be kissed when we struck our bargain. And I'm going start with your lovely breasts."

She simply blinked and blushed, but didn't move.

Patience. This is monumental for her. But his cock was so full, and heavy. He'd be able to proceed slower if he wasn't in such exquisite agony.

Joseph reached out and grasped the yellow ribbon resting so temptingly between her tits. Moving matters along, he pulled it loose. Her eyes widened. Her hand shot out and grabbed his wrist.

"It's all right. You came here for this . . . Let me give you the pleasure you seek." Her hand still on his wrist, he opened the fastenings on her gown, his experienced fingers making quick work of it. She looked unsure, wanting to continue as much as she wanted to stop him. But thankfully, she didn't pull his hand away.

She may be a virgin but she was no innocent. She was too well read on the subject of sex not to know exactly what his intentions were once the gown was opened. It kept her riveted. It stopped her from stopping him. Her breaths were quickening once more.

When at last he reached her chemise, she tensed. Joseph paused. Rumors he'd heard about her disfigured body raced through his mind. He shoved them aside, unconcerned, and gave the final article a quick downward yank.

No scarring or burns. Simply two perfect breasts and the prettiest pink nipples he'd ever seen.

Her gaze was fixed on his face, observing his reaction closely.

He took his time to take in the sight before him. With her pale blond curls sensuously mussed, the front of her gown open, and the neckline of her chemise tucked under her breasts, she was pure sexual allure.

The goddess of temptation—who could lure men to their misfortune.

He swore softly. "You look like every man's fantasy."

Her eyes softened and her delicate shoulders relaxed.

He caressed the outer curve of one soft mound. "I think it's time we started experiencing some fantasies together. Wouldn't you say?"

She shivered. Not from fear, or cold, but from anticipation and excitement. All this pent-up passion was his for the unleashing. How fortunate was he?

Her nipples protruded, so tempting and tantalizing, begging to be sucked. He knew she thought he was going to go straight to kissing those luscious buds. Instead Joseph pinched one excited little tip. She cried out and grabbed his biceps, startled by the keen sensation. He held the sensitive teat firmly, applying just enough pressure, letting it build into scintillating throbs.

Her head fell back against the wall. For his efforts, she gave him a long hearty moan he felt down to the tip of his cock.

Leaning in, he brought his mouth to her ear. "In our carnal encounters, we'll only do what we both like." Gently, he pulled and rolled the tender tip of her breast with expert finesse, purposely plying her with a steady stream of erotic sensations. He loved the sounds of her short sharp pants. "I know I'm enjoying this. Tell me, *ma belle*, how does this feel? You like this, don't you, Emilie." It was more of a statement than a question, given her sensual reactions.

He straightened and looked at her, his fingers never relenting on the captive bud. She leaned heavily against the wall, her breathing labored, her eyes closed. All she could do was nod. Her skin was flushed and a pretty blond curl had fallen onto her cheek. His heart raced as he watched her in her wanton state. He had to come so badly his sac hurt. But he couldn't stop what he was doing. Seeing the untamed desire on her face was rapture in itself.

He'd imagined her like this more times than he could count.

Releasing her nipple, he captured the other between his finger and thumb and pinched, giving it the same carnal treatment. She lurched and moaned louder, her fingers digging into his arms.

"Are you ready for your kiss, Emilie?"

"Oh God . . . Yes . . . *Please* . . ." Each word breathless.

A sweet plea no man could resist.

Still holding her nipple captive, Joseph cupped her other breast with his free hand and sucked the tip into his mouth. She gasped and arched, her fingers tangling in his hair.

The taste of the pebbled nipple in his mouth spiked his hunger. He was starved for more. He wanted her complete surrender. No hesitations. No inhibitions. No will to deny him anything. Pure unbridled abandon. He licked and sucked at her breast, treating her other nipple to tender twists and tugs. The double stimulation had her writhing against the wall, tightening her fingers in his hair, the sensuous sounds she made inciting him further.

Famished, he turned and latched on to the other breast, his hands now holding her soft mounds up high, his greedy mouth laving and lightly biting the savory teat, feeding off her frenzy. He felt light-headed with lust. His body screamed for release.

Merde. He was *actually* shaking.

He tore his mouth away, swept her up in his arms, and stalked toward the bed. He tossed her onto the mattress; she landed with a bounce and a squeak. His blood pounded in his veins. She had him so undone, all he could think about was driving his cock into her cunt.

She rose to her elbows, her tempting nipples erect and wet from his mouth. Joseph tore his justacorps off and threw the knee-length coat to the floor. His vest followed. Reaching for the fastenings on his breeches, he opened them, yanked his shirt free, and discarded it.

Slowly, her gaze moved down his bare chest to his engorged shaft straining out of the breeches. Her tactile perusal made him harder and bigger. He'd never been this painfully large, his cock feeling hard as stone and as heavy as lead. Gripping the base tightly, he stroked his prick, trying to ease the discomfort.

Engrossed in his actions, she watched intently.

"You see what you do to my cock, Emilie? Does it excite you to see me aroused for you?"

She had a pretty blush to her cheeks. It made her blond hair look even paler and her green eyes more vibrant. "It amazes me . . . and thrills me and . . . Yes, it . . . arouses me."

God, she was as adorable as she was seductive. He doubted she knew just how soft and sultry her voice sounded.

"You want my cock inside you, don't you?"

She nodded. "Yes, I want it. I want it all . . . Every physical pleasure you can bestow. I want all of it."

Oh, he was going to give her all of it. She was going to take every inch of his aching shaft. He was going to ride her to what he knew was going to be an explosive release. For both of them.

The carnal fire burning between them practically crackled in the air.

"Pull up your gown and remove your drawers for me. Show me your pretty cunt."

"You want me to—" She faltered. The concept of revealing herself for him was clearly still an obstacle.

"Pull up your skirts and bunch them up against your belly. Do it." He hadn't meant for his tone to be so sharp, but he was hanging on to his control by a thread. And it was quickly unraveling. He squeezed the swollen head of his cock to combat the throbbing.

She looked down at her gown and bit her lush bottom lip.

Joseph reached out and grasped her shoes. Pulling them off, he dropped them to the floor and said, "You want it all. That's what I wish to give you. To make the experience all it can be. I want to give you all the pleasure you deserve, *ma belle*." He'd told a lot of lies in the boudoir over the years, but he meant every word. "I know you were planning on being taken by a masked lover, doing no more than hiking up your skirts and having him fill you, sight unseen. You're not limited to encounters like that. You can have a much more intimate sexual experience. Allow yourself to experience it with me."

There would be no barriers when she was with him. He was going to level every one of them, and the misconceptions she had about her form and appeal. Even if it killed him. And given his state, it just might.

Her chest rose and fell with her rapid breaths. She made no other movement. And it didn't look as though she would.

She needs more coaxing. He'd try a different approach.

Joseph sank one knee into the mattress and then the other. "Very well. If you're not comfortable, we'll do it your way. I'll pull up your gown. I won't look. I'll take you through the slit in your drawers." He grabbed the hem of her skirts, praying she'd object to the suggestion. The thought of taking her that way sank his heart.

"No, wait." Her hand shot out.

Joseph released the hem immediately. She sat up, took a deep breath, then to his delight, grasped handfuls of fabric and began sliding the gown up her legs, pulling the voluminous layers up to her belly. Bunching the fabrics against her, she reached down for the ties on her caleçons.

Riveted, his gaze followed the actions of her nimble fingers as she loosened the ties, slipped the linen drawers off her bottom, and slid them down her legs. He grabbed hold of them when they reached her knees and pulled them off the rest of the way. She still had her stockings on, but he didn't care. He was transfixed by the lovely—unmarred—skin above her knees and the small patch of dark blond curls he could see between her legs, just below the fabrics of her skirts.

Wrapping his fingers around her ankles, he bent her knees, setting her feet down on the bed well apart. "Don't close your knees," he said when he saw them drifting together. "Lie back."

Clearly growing bolder, she only hesitated for a moment or two before acquiescing, though she watched his every move.

Her sex was open to him for his viewing pleasure. She was wet for him, her opening dripping with her essence, making her pretty pink flesh glisten and the light-colored curls between her legs damp with her juices.

Lightly, he grazed his fingers between the warm slick folds. With a cry, she all but lifted off the bed. She was so ripe for the taking. So primed, a few strokes over her clit would send her into orgasm.

And he refused to do it. She was going to come with him inside her first.

Leaning over her, he pressed his palm on the mattress near her head. His other hand gently massaged her soaked sex, not enough to make her come, just enough to keep her focus there and feed the fever. "You want to come for me, don't you, Emilie?" This little virgin knew exactly what he was talking about. In her letters, she'd boldly asked him a dozen questions about sexual climax.

Fisting the coverlet, she closed her eyes with a moan and arched into his hand. Her nipples were an appealing distraction. They were jutting out, needing to be kissed and sucked again.

"Answer me, Emilie."

"Yes! Yes, I want to . . . come."

He slid a finger inside her. She gasped and squirmed. He groaned.

A single digit was all he had in her and it was firmly clasped in her hot satiny sheath, the tight sensation mind-numbing. His cock twitched with anticipation. He couldn't wait to have her. If she hadn't been a virgin, he would have been buried to the hilt by now. Joseph eased his finger out and slid two back in. She squirmed a little harder as he gently stretched her. Sweat broke out on his brow.

"Please . . . I need . . ." Her words melted into a whimper when he withdrew his fingers.

He knew exactly what she needed. He needed a fucking release, too. He'd never needed any woman this badly, but her damned virginity couldn't be forgotten. Intent on stretching her tight little sheath beforehand, he wanted to minimize her discomfort, hurt her as little as possible when he entered her. "I'll let you come very soon. I swear it."

He lowered himself beside her and swooped in for a kiss, devouring her lush mouth. Penetrating her with his tongue. He feasted on her taste, forcing her mouth to open wider to accommodate his possession. His hand was back to caressing her sex, wet silky folds he couldn't stop touching, letting his palm lightly scrape over her clit on occasion, purposely giving her a constant spike of sensations. Throwing her arms around his neck, she mewed with each rhythmic stroke, her legs now sprawled open on the bed, no longer bent or tense.

Just the way he liked it.

He slid three fingers into her. With a lurch, she recoiled and tried to squirm away, but with his body half covering hers, and the material to her skirts caught under him, she didn't get far.

Pushing and pulling his fingers in and out, he turned to her nipple and drew it into his mouth, taking her focus away from the intrusion of his hand, to the sensations of his tongue. He continued to work her with his fingers, with his mouth, until he had her arching to him once more and moaning loudly. Three fingers didn't come close to how thick he was at the moment, but it was going to have to be enough, because he'd reached the end of his rope.

Pulling his hand out, he slid his slick fingers down his cock, coating it with her cream for easy penetration. He was so far gone, he wasn't certain how gentle he'd be.

He was on her in an instant, pinning her down, spreading her thighs with his knees.

"Say you want me to take you," he demanded, wedging his cock against her opening, his chest heaving with the exertion it took not to give in to the lure of her wet sex and drive into her.

"I want you, Vinc—" He crushed his mouth to hers, silencing her with a hot hard kiss. *Jésus-Christ*. His brother's name was the last thing he wanted to hear from her lips at the moment.

"Tell me you want the man you exchange letters with. The one who knows you better than any other man. Tell me you want that man. He's the one you want to surrender to." What the hell was he doing? Why did any of this matter a whit? Especially *now*. *She's begging to be taken.* He should be fucking her. Forget the rest!

"Yes . . . you're the one I want," she said.

He had her mouth, his kiss a mix of savage hunger and alarming desperation.

There was no easy way to do this except quickly. Joseph plunged into her.

Hot pleasure roared through him; a cry erupted from her. He closed his eyes and clenched his teeth. The pressure around his cock was spine-melting, his thickened prick pulsing sharply inside the tight confines of her cunt. The sweetest torture.

Emilie's face was buried in his neck, her arms squeezing him fiercely.

"Are you all right?" he said in her ear, his voice more a rasp than a whisper. He felt her nod. Sweet little liar. Her body was rigid and tense. She wasn't all right.

"Try to relax. Almost there." He was halfway.

At that, her head jerked up. "Almost?"

He withdrew a little, and then drove back in, this time sinking his cock completely. She bit her lip and gave a strangled cry.

Pure pleasure exploded through his senses.

Nothing in heaven could be finer than this. He'd never been inside any woman who felt this good. Never experienced the intense sensations radiating up his cock. He reared then slowly tunneled back into the snug honeyed heat. The friction along the sensitive underside of his cock was magnificent. He thrust in again, and again, the most stunning sensations flooding through him. It took him several moments before he noted her body drawn up tight; he could tell she was holding her breath. "Look at me, Emilie," he said.

She looked up at him, her eyes watery.

Joseph brushed an errant curl off her soft cheek, slowing down his pace. "It's done, *ma belle*. Breathe through it. The discomfort will pass. There's only pleasure from now on." He kissed her luscious mouth and gave her perfect sheath more strokes of his cock, fighting back his release, basking in the vast pleasure of each plunge and drag.

She was beginning to relax, her body yielding. Returning his heated kiss, growing hungrier.

Shifting his body, he changed his angle and picked up the tempo. "*Dieu*, that feels good. So good. You feel that?" She concurred with a whimper. Her hips jerked up and down until at last she found her rhythm. If he could have smiled, he would have. He knew it wouldn't take her long. She was too naturally, deliciously hot-blooded not to be swept up. She was made for a man's pleasure. For his pleasure.

You're mine . . .

Joseph hooked his arm under her knee and brought her leg up, his thrusts harder and faster now, making constant contact with her sensitive clit. "Page eight . . ." he murmured to her.

She was frantic now, driving her hips up to meet each solid thrust, her body reaching for him over and over again.

"That's it. That's perfect," he growled. The most glorious tremors rippled along the feminine muscles, gripping his thrusting cock. A bead of sweat rolled down his back.

He could feel Emilie's fingers digging into his shoulders, her sweet sex creaming around his cock, bathing his shaft. She was so slick, her essence trickled onto his sac. The sensation drove him wild. *Seigneur Dieu.* She was the sweetest fuck he'd ever had. He loved how perfect the passion was. How deliciously she'd surrendered to it. To him. Her every sensual reaction unpracticed, untamed, and beyond her control. It was inebriating. It made his mind spin.

She squeezed down around him. The sudden clench tore a groan from his throat. She was on the edge of orgasm. He'd never emptied himself inside a woman, but with his sac so full of come and the need to let go so immense, he braced himself for her release.

It came immediately. Her hips shot up with her scream, throwing her head back. He rammed her for all he was worth, riding her as she contracted around his prick, milking him. Barely able to hold back his orgasm, he wouldn't pull out. Didn't want to. He was gluttonous for more. Intent on remaining inside her as long as he could, he held on by sheer iron will.

Then her body gave him a squeeze, followed by another final clench and his orgasm slammed into him. Semen bubbled up from his sac and shot down his cock. He barely pulled out in time, rearing onto his knees, fisting the counterpane with both hands near her head, just as hot blasts of come erupted out of him and onto her belly and thigh. Ecstasy washed through him. He bellowed out his bliss, purging his cock in thick steady streams, his muscles melting with each powerful spurt that pour from his prick.

His release went on and on. He floated in euphoria, until he'd completely emptied his cock with a final shuddering drop.

On all fours, sucking in gulps of air, he looked down at her.

Her lovely flaxen curls were fanned out haphazardly around her head. With her gown open at the front, he could see that a soft pink blush had colored her skin from her cheeks to her breasts. Her beautiful nipples were still erect.

She was a vision.

The most gorgeous one he'd ever seen.

She gazed back at him, a small smile on her face, and in her eyes he saw something akin to joy. Funny, but he was feeling much the same way. It had to be the incredible climax he'd just had that inspired the sentiment. In fact, he felt more than joy. He felt great. Better than ever. A unique sense of deep contentment he'd never known after sex seeped into his marrow.

Joseph leaned down and gave her lush mouth a soft kiss. "Don't move." He snagged her caleçons, and wiped her belly and thigh clean. "You're not going to need these anyway. Not for the rest of the week." He smiled.

It was only when he grabbed the base of his sex that he noticed it wasn't coated with just her juices and his come. There were traces of blood. Her virginity. A stark reminder of what had just happened. He'd claimed her maidenhead. Quickly he wiped himself clean, rose off the bed on shaky legs, and tossed the garment to the floor for the servants, hoping Emilie hadn't seen the blood, concerned the sight might upset her.

He didn't want her to have any remorse over her lost innocence or regret over the encounter.

He cleaned himself at the water basin then returned to the bed with a damp clean cloth.

Stretching out beside her, he propped himself on one elbow and pressed the cool cloth to her sex. She flinched.

"Tender?" he asked. He'd been too rough for her first time, despite his best intentions, but he couldn't help it. She'd driven him into practical delirium.

She caressed his cheek and kissed him. "I'm fine. I don't care about the tenderness or the loss of innocence. Or for that matter, the blood you were trying to hide from me. I knew to expect it." Of course she did. His enlightened virgin. The only virgin he'd ever paid any attention to, much less bedded.

The only woman to hold his interest for a year. An unprecedented feat.

"I will cherish this experience, in fact, everything we do together as lovers this week," she said. "I loved every moment of this night. And I've developed an immense fondness for page eight." Her smile drew one from him as well.

He lightly brushed the cloth over her clit, making her gasp. "There are other pages waiting to earn your regard."

She laughed. "And I look forward to them with great eagerness and anticipation." She pressed her mouth to his once more. He returned her kiss. A long, languorous, delicious kiss.

"Thank you," she whispered against his lips. "You made my first experience wonderful. I'm glad it was you, Vincent."

Joseph flinched, the reality of the situation hitting him hard. She'd never know the man she'd been with was him. He could never tell her any more than he could reveal his other deceptions.

And he hated it.

Hated it that he'd be her lover for the rest of the week and she'd never once scream his name in pleasure. And he'd no idea why the notion bothered him at all. He and his brother had been switching places all of their lives—the boudoir included. They looked so much alike that, since childhood, even their nurse had had trouble telling them apart.

This was the first time he'd ever pretended to be Vincent yet wanted to reveal the truth.

But the truth would devastate her. Worse, it would diminish the encounter for her. He couldn't stand that thought either. He would give her everything she wanted and more this week. He'd make her see in herself what he saw in her—that she was gorgeous and extraordinary. Then he'd back away at week's end.

Because of what had happened between them tonight, it was more important than ever to maintain his ruse.

Bedding her had complicated matters. And raised the stakes. The amount of pain he'd cause her if she learned the truth was even greater. Moreover, it had done nothing—absolutely nothing—to sate his lust for her.

She snuggled closer; the scent of lavender caressed his senses. Silky blond curls brushed his jaw as she trailed warm kisses down his neck, her soft breasts pressing against his bare chest. Joseph closed his eyes and pulled her tightly into his arms.

He wanted her again. Had to have her again.

There was no way he could resist her and walk away now.

There was no way he'd let Vincent or any man in attendance at this gathering have her.

He had mere days to get his fill of Emilie so he wouldn't long for her afterward. He wouldn't continue the affair beyond the week.

CHAPTER FIVE

"Good morning." Emilie walked into her aunt's private apartments the next day smiling and sat down at the table with Pauline and Marthe in the antechamber. Her presence in the room had effectively silenced the two older women's bickering. Arguing that could be heard from the hallway.

The subject of their argument was Emilie. As always. But she was in too fine a mood to be aggravated.

A servant stepped forward to pour her a goblet of water with orange slices. Reaching for the crystal vessel, Emilie brought it to her lips and stopped short when she saw the looks of shock on her mealtime companions' faces.

"Is there something amiss?" she asked and took a sip.

"Why, Emilie . . ." Marthe began. "You're not wearing a cloak."

"And it isn't morning. It's midday," her aunt was quick to point out.

Emilie motioned the servant to place two slices of ham on her plate as well as a hearty portion of mutton. Normally she didn't much care for mutton and gravy, but she was famished. She'd yet to break the fast.

"I'm afraid I slept in," she said to her aunt and to Marthe. "I don't believe I need a cloak today, dear Marthe. It's rather warm." As a habit, she'd placed one on earlier, but even the lightest of the lot felt heavy and cumbersome. She'd walked out of her rooms in simply her gown, feeling light and free and entirely different. Thanks to Vincent. She even felt . . . well, pretty.

He'd made her feel desirable. He'd made her feel desire, delicious and pure. He'd made her feel like a woman. Whole. Undamaged. Not for a moment in his arms did she feel in any way less than any other female. She hadn't had to hide her identity. He wanted her. Just as she was. And that alone made it impossible to deny what she'd been trying to suppress for many months. She was in love with him. Rather hopelessly, actually.

She wasn't naïve enough to think Vincent was going to propose marriage or that his affections ran as deeply as hers.

The prudent thing to do in this situation was to guard her vulnerable heart and leave promptly, sparing herself the anguish it was going to be to part with him at the end of the week. With certainty, the longer she stayed with him, the greater the heartache.

But she refused to leave—heartache be damned. She wouldn't deprive herself of the opportunity to be with him. That way, in her old age she couldn't bemoan how she'd missed out on an incredible week, on creating cherished memories—all because she'd lacked the courage to face the heartbreak and had run.

Vincent had kept her up until the early morning hours making love. She wouldn't deny herself of more of the same. Heated memories flitted through her mind. She felt her nipples harden and her heart dance. There was a delicious soreness to her private muscles that reminded her of the magical night she'd had— one that hadn't required any make-believe at all.

Cutting into the ham, Emilie looked up.

Pauline's surprise was turning into a large grin, Marthe's astonishment quickly becoming horror.

"You had a man last night!" they said in chorus.

Emilie glanced over at the elderly servant. The man looked ancient and perhaps hard of hearing, but still . . . She was hesitant to speak.

Her aunt impatiently waved the servant away. Only when he'd gone did she place her hand on Emilie's arm. "It was the man outside in the corridor, wasn't it?"

Emilie couldn't suppress her smile. "It was."

"I want to hear everything!" Pauline beamed.

Marthe shook her head. "I want to hear none of it."

"Hush, Marthe." Her aunt patted Emilie's arm. "Did your lover please you, *chérie?*"

Emilie's smile broadened. "He did. Immensely." He did more than please her. Seeing herself through his eyes had bolstered the confidence she'd lost in herself. Had made her heart soar.

Jubilation erupted out of Pauline with a joyful squeak. "Ah, this is wonderful!"

"Wonderful? She gives herself to a nameless man, forfeiting her—"

"Not another word," Pauline cut off Marthe's rant. Her aunt's smile returned as she gazed at Emilie. "Look at her. She's lovely—all aglow after a night of passion. She has needs and longings, just like any woman—except you, Marthe. It isn't right or healthy for her to remain secluded. Or deprived of physical love. It's the most wonderful thing in the world. And yet women are too often denied, trapped in unsatisfying marriages. While men have their mistresses, most of them openly without discretion, a woman must be discreet if she takes a lover or abstain all together. Society tries to discourage women from indulging our physical yearnings while men are encouraged to satisfy theirs. It is because of this terrible injustice I have these gatherings. Women know they can come here, regardless of their circumstance, and are safe to partake. Without judgment. And with complete anonymity."

"Yes, quite the charitable work you're doing," Marthe injected blandly.

Pauline ignored her and continued, her smile still in place. "I am delighted you tasted passion with a skilled lover, *chérie.*"

"Thank you, Aunt." Emilie looked at Marthe. "He was not nameless, Marthe. I knew exactly who he was."

"Yes, we both do! I recognized him immediately, despite the mask. Some men are just so sinfully potent, they stand out of the crowd," Pauline said. "Marthe, I'll have you know that our darling Emilie was with none other than one of the Duc de Vernant's very handsome sons."

At that, Marthe's posture straightened, her eyes widening. "You were? A member of the house of Alumbert?"

"Yes, it's true." Emilie confirmed. Her smile had yet to leave her face. She could hardly wait to see him again, her body famished for his touch. His mouth. His body inside hers.

She didn't know a man could give a woman so much joy and pleasure.

"I must say, I was rather surprised who you selected, *chérie*, but"—Pauline shrugged—"if he pleased you, then I am pleased."

"Who was it?" Marthe asked. "Which one? Gilbert?"

Emilie laughed. "No, not him. I was with—"

"Joseph," Pauline responded.

"Vincent," Emilie quickly corrected her aunt.

Pauline frowned. "*Vincent?* Really? Are you certain?"

"Of course I'm certain. Vincent and I have been corresponding for the last year. I know him quite well."

"She'd never be with Joseph d'Alumbert," Marthe added. "Or any of his equally unappealing friends—who hang on his every word and follow him about as if he were the King himself. He may be the heir to a dukedom but he and his companions are a horrid lot."

Pauline still looked confused. "I was so certain that was Joseph . . ."

"Well, it wasn't, rest assured," Emilie said. "I couldn't agree with Marthe's opinion more."

"Yes, why do you permit such men here?" Marthe asked. "Especially after the way they treated Emilie."

Pauline stiffened. "I may not like the man or his friends, but you know as well as I do that one does not forbid a member of the Duc de Vernant's family from attending any gathering."

It was true. Doors were flung open for the Duc's heir and those he favored. It felt wonderfully empowering to turn down one of Joseph's friends last eve—his mask unable to conceal his boorish manners. He was easily recognized.

Just one of the many who had behaved so heartlessly that night years ago.

Imagine how delightful it would be to rebuff Joseph—just as she'd done to his friend?

While she was here, she wouldn't deny herself that experience either. It was time someone brought him down a notch. Or two. She wasn't going to run or hide from Joseph or anyone. Anymore. Given the sheer abundance of decadent behavior and enthusiasm as people roamed about looking for their next carnal diversion, she was sure to run into Joseph.

It was inevitable.

She'd look him in the eye. And then give him the cut direct.

*****

"Wake up." Gilbert gave Joseph a jarring shake.

Joseph sat bolt up, startled out of a deep sleep. He'd been dreaming of a sweet seductress with flaxen hair, captivating moss green eyes, and the most divine lips—as enchanting as the princesses in the fables he'd been told as a child.

Only this princess was in his bed. She belonged to *him*. Gave herself to him, wanted only him, engulfed him in the most sublime passion he'd ever tasted.

But the fair princess had been torn from his sight only to be replaced by Gilbert's face.

Joseph frowned. "What the hell are you doing here?" He raked a hand through his hair.

"Well, good day to you, too, dear brother. I see you're in a good mood. You could show some gratitude, you know. I could have let you sleep and miss out on the afternoon and evening festivities. I've been at the Basset table all afternoon. Strip Basset." Gilbert grinned. "I won. Joseph, you should have been there. A woman with the finest tits you've ever seen sat—"

Joseph grabbed a fistful of Gilbert's justacorps and yanked him closer. "What do you mean 'miss out on the afternoon and evening festivities'? What time is it?"

Releasing Gilbert, Joseph glanced past his brother at the tall windows. By the low summer sun, he realized the day was old.

"It's almost supper time, but if you hurry, you can squeeze in some amusements beforehand—"

"Merde." He'd been with Emilie until almost dawn. After their delicious night of ecstasy, of sexual excess, he'd slept so deeply, so soundly. And for so damned long. None of this would have happened if she'd let him stay. He was certain that with her by his side, he would have awakened once she stirred.

After sex, he normally left, and yet last eve he had no desire to leave her side. A first. She'd turned him away—albeit ever so sweetly. Another first. He usually departed the boudoir with the woman begging him to remain. But he knew why she'd refused.

It was too uncomfortable to sleep in her gown and she wasn't ready to remove it for him. He'd decided not to press her. He'd coax the gown and the rest of her clothing off her soon enough. Tremendous strides had already been made in the few short hours they'd been together. He'd seen her blossom sexually before his eyes, her inhibitions lower.

Adorable yet mouthwateringly sensuous Emilie de Sarron had been his perfect sexual match throughout the night—inciting the sweetest heat no man could resist.

He was hard at the thought of being back in her silky sex, all warm and wet and fisted so tightly around him.

"Since you're up, I'll return to the amusements below. Why leave Vincent to have all the fun."

Joseph's heart lurched. "Vincent?" His brother's name tumbled from his lips on a breath.

Gilbert smoothed his justacorps. "Yes. Vincent. Your twin. Remember him? I haven't seen him in hours. No doubt he's found the lady with the cloak he's been looking for and is enjoying some rapturous delights as we speak." Gilbert smiled.

Joseph tore out of bed.

*****

Emilie moved through the grand vestibule slowly, squeezing her way through the crush of people. Searching for Vincent.

It seemed as though there were even more guests in attendance this night than the night before. She held on to the train of her gown, lest someone stomp on it.

She'd bathed and primped that afternoon, anxiously preparing to see Vincent again. And after much consideration, she'd finally selected her masquerade attire for this eve from the various costumes she'd brought. A cream-colored demi-mask garnished with small to medium light brown plumes ensured her anonymity and matched her gown.

It, too, was cream-colored and had a light brown overskirt that was drawn back to encircle her hips, cascading into a long train behind her. The very end of her train was a soft red. And on her gown were large brown and cream bell-shaped sleeves. Very much like the wings of a bird.

Her attire representative of just that very thing—a bird.

One of her favorites.

A little bird that was rather plain. Upon first glance, it wouldn't likely garner a second. But what made this creature special came from within. And she liked that. As much as she liked the sound of the bird's nocturnal crescendos.

This eve, Emilie was a nightingale.

She finally made it into the long corridor that led to the dining hall. That was when she spotted him. Vincent. Or perhaps it was Joseph.

He was just ahead, moving with the crowd. Wearing a brown justacorps and black breeches, his tall chiseled form, his strong shoulders were eye-catching; his masculine beauty made him stand out at any gathering.

Her pulse quickened. She quickened her pace.

Clutching her train tightly in her hand, she negotiated around the people who walked between her and the ever-nearing d'Alumbert ahead. Anticipation building with each rapid step that brought her closer to him.

Which one was he?

Her instincts told her—Vincent.

But it didn't matter, really. She had good reason to stop either.

The moment he got within arm's length, she reached out and caught his hand, arresting his steps.

He turned to face her. She noted the surprise that momentarily flashed in his eyes, despite his brown-and-black-checkered mask.

"Vincent?" she blurted out softly as people pressed past.

His sinfully tempting mouth lifted in a slow seductive smile. "Yes?"

Emilie felt a surge of joy. She clasped both his hands and backed up, pulling him with her away from the center of the hallway where they were being bumped by the boisterous lot streaming past. She stopped short when her back met the wall.

She couldn't contain her grin. "I've been looking for you."

Releasing her hands, he pressed his palms against the wall on either side of her head. "Have you, now. Well, then . . . I'm glad you found me, *chérie*."

There was something about the way he spoke, or perhaps it was in the way he looked at her . . . Something was not quite right.

Emilie dismissed it as absurd.

He was likely putting on a bit of a performance, given the very public place they stood in and all the ears that moved past. She knew he'd do whatever it took to protect her anonymity. She trusted him explicitly.

"I'm absolutely famished," she told him.

"Famished?" It wasn't what he was expecting her to say.

"Yes, for Vincent d'Alumbert's delectable kisses." Smiling, she tilted her chin up a notch, bringing her lips closer to his irresistible mouth. "Kiss me."

Chapter Six

"With pleasure . . ." Vincent murmured just before his lips met Emilie's eager mouth.

Grasping her chin, he held her face captive, angled, as he slanted his mouth over hers. Impatient for more, she parted her lips for him.

He didn't hesitate to slide his tongue inside.

Something was . . . different. His kiss felt different. The way he kissed her . . . heated, yes, but with a certain detachment and distance she hadn't felt from him the night before.

And where was "it"? The bolt of hot excitement that rocked her every time he touched her, kissed her. Or even neared.

This was the man she'd surrendered her innocence to and had spent a night and morning of rapture in his arms. She'd shared intimacies with him—on many levels.

Yet, this kiss didn't feel at all intimate.

Suddenly his mouth and the press of his hard body were gone and a growled oath shot out of him.

She snapped her eyes open and gasped.

Vincent's twin brother, Joseph, stood beside them. The firm grip on Vincent's arm and the angry frown on Vincent's mouth told her instantly that Joseph had yanked him away.

"I need to speak to you," Joseph said to his twin, his jaw tight. Though half his face was covered by his dark blue mask, she could tell he was fuming.

"I'm busy at the moment, in case it isn't obvious." Vincent kept his tone light but his voice was strained, clearly struggling with his ire.

"Now," Joseph said, the word sharply dealt.

For a moment the two large men stared at each other in muted fury. But then, Vincent took a deep breath and let it out slowly. "Very well. This had better be urgent."

Before Vincent could offer her a single word, Joseph pointed a finger at Emilie. "You, stay here. Don't move from this spot. Vincent will return shortly." It was an order. Rather an odd one coming from Joseph. She couldn't imagine why he'd care if a woman waited for Vincent or not.

Dumbstruck, she watched the brothers disappear into the crowd.

*****

On opening the fourth door in the long hallway, Joseph finally found a room that wasn't occupied by couples fucking.

Stepping inside the library, he was livid. Seething. His very entrails twisting in his gut over an emotion he'd never felt in his life. One he didn't even believe he was capable of feeling—until Emilie came along. The ridiculous, possessive emotion had torn through him the moment he saw Vincent in a heated exchange with her.

Vincent stopped in the middle of the room, ripped off his mask, and turned to face Joseph. "What was so important you had to interrupt me just now?"

Joseph was just closing the door when Gilbert pushed his way inside, a typical grin on his face. He grabbed a chair, sat down, and pulled off his mask. "I saw what just happened in the corridor. I don't want to miss any of this," he said cheerfully.

Joseph held back the few choice words he had for his youngest brother, shut the door, and locked it. His focus at the moment was his twin.

"So? Are you going to tell me what you want, Joseph?" Vincent asked.

Joseph pulled off his mask. "Yes. I want your clothes. Take them off."

"*My clothes?*"

"That's correct. Remove them."

Vincent crossed his arms. "When did it happen?"

"When did what happen?"

"When did you take complete leave of your senses?"

Gilbert laughed but instantly sobered when Joseph shot him a glare. Averting his gaze to the ceiling, Gilbert feigned sudden interest in its mural.

"Vincent . . ." Joseph strove for calm, trying to mask the extent of his discomposure over the incident in the hallway around his brothers. The ridicule would be endless if they had any idea how it had affected him. As it was, he was stunned by how strongly he wanted to slam his fist into his brother's belly for kissing Emilie. The image of Vincent's mouth on hers was still boiling his blood. He shouldn't be this riled. Not after all the women he and Vincent had shared. "Either you remove your attire or I will remove it for you."

Vincent raked a hand through his hair. "Clearly, by your request for my clothing, you want someone to believe you're me. Fine. I don't care. Let me finish with the woman in the hallway and then the clothing is all yours."

"No!" Joseph cringed at how strongly that came out. "You're not having the woman in the hallway." He'd managed to lower his voice and keep his tone quiet and even.

"*Dieu.* Joseph, what has gotten into you? First you lay claim on the lady in the cloak and now this wo—" His twin stopped mid-word. Then a wolfish smile formed on his face. "The lady in the cloak is this woman. Isn't she?"

Merde.

"Well, well . . ." Gilbert rose snickering, walked over to stand beside Vincent, and casually propped his elbow on Vincent's shoulder. "Aside from the tantalizing tidbits of his time spent with the fair lady, I think Joseph is keeping a great deal from his brothers, wouldn't you agree, Vincent?"

"I would indeed, Gilbert."

They were both smiling at him, thoroughly enjoying themselves.

He didn't want to punch Vincent anymore. He wanted to punch both his brothers.

"So, Joseph, are you going to tell us who the lady is, once and for all?" Vincent prompted.

"No."

"Very well. I have a lovely nightingale who is waiting for me. Warmed and wet." Vincent took a step toward the door.

Joseph stood in his path. "I'm not done with her yet. And she isn't warm and wet for you. Her stirrings are for me."

Vincent patted Joseph on the shoulder. "I'm fine with that. By the way, she did say she was *famished* for Vincent d'Alumbert's kisses. I'm happy to finish what you started."

Joseph pressed his hand firmly against Vincent's chest to discourage any progress. "You're not having her."

"Can I have her?" Gilbert asked.

Joseph's gaze jerked to his younger sibling. "Not another word from you."

Gilbert's eyes widened, affecting an innocent look. "I was only trying to help—you know, break the impasse?" His lips twitched. He was fighting back a smile.

Joseph turned to Vincent and caught him holding back his mirth as well. *Merde.* They were playing with him. Purposely trying to push him into showing his sorry state.

Both his brothers burst out laughing. "I never thought the day would come when Joseph had a *tendre* for a lady," Vincent said.

"You're mad." Something deep inside Joseph balked at the protest.

Chuckling, Gilbert said, "I've just got to know who she is now."

"Me, too. I've never seen you so possessive over any other female. We're your brothers, Joseph. We've never kept any secrets from each other. Who is she? And why didn't you use your own name instead of mine?"

"I can't use my name. Leave it at that."

"Not enough of an answer," Vincent pressed. His brothers stared back, still sporting their foolish grins. Sensing his discomfort, they were reveling in it. Clearly, they weren't going to relent until they got their answers.

"Look, she's not like the other women here. She's never done this sort of thing," Joseph said.

"Never done what sort of thing? Attended one of the Comtesse's gatherings? Or—"

"Fucked?" Gilbert finished Vincent's sentence.

Joseph let out a sharp sigh. "Both. There. Is that enough for you?"

If he wasn't so frustrated, he might have laughed. The looks on his siblings' faces, wide eyes and gaping mouths, were comical.

"The woman in the cloak is . . . was a virgin? You had a . . . *virgin?*" Gilbert asked.

"Since when have you ever been interested in deflowering women?" Vincent was clearly incredulous, too.

Since he met Emilie. A woman who took his breath away at every turn. And had him behaving in ways he'd never conceived. He couldn't wait to join the beautiful nightingale waiting for him in the corridor. All he wanted to do was to possess that snug wet heat once more and ride her in more sexual positions from her erotic volume. Last night he'd delighted in satisfying her sexual curiosity and basked in the mind-numbing pleasure it was to fuck her.

The mere thought of having her again made him rock hard.

But he first had to get his brothers under control.

He never wanted to have to peel one of them off Emilie again.

"I hadn't planned on having her initially. It just happened," was his weak explanation.

"Good Lord, you've been trapped!" Vincent's expression had turned to alarm. "She's going to tell her family and you, dear brother, are going to be hauled to the altar."

"That's not going to happen."

"Of course it's going to happen! You're the heir to a dukedom." Vincent began to pace. "We'll say you were with us. That the lady is lying or mistaken and——"

"Well, actually, she thinks you deflowered her, *Vincent*. You're the one who would be hauled to the altar." Joseph's words arrested Vincent's steps. For the first time since entering the room, Joseph felt a smile coming on.

Vincent's expression was one of abject horror.

"Me?! That's why you used my name? So you wouldn't be trapped?"

Joseph chuckled. "Be at ease, Vincent. I assure you she has absolutely no such intentions."

"Was the tumble any good?" Gilbert asked.

Both Joseph and Vincent shot him a look.

"What?" Gilbert said to Vincent. "You're not curious?"

Vincent turned to Joseph. "Actually, I am. Was it any good?"

His greedy cock gave an instant hungry throb. "It was heaven."

The best he ever had.

"A virgin? Really?" Gilbert pondered the notion.

"So why not take credit for the tumble?" Vincent asked. "Just who is this woman? Since you're using my name, you could at the very least tell me."

Joseph stared silently at his brothers. As much as they needled him——and it was going to be incessant over this——he knew they wouldn't relay any information he gave them to anyone else. Perhaps if he enlisted their help, it might make it easier to get through the week?

If he didn't count the nerve-grating, aggravating ribbing he was going to endure from them.

Joseph drew in a breath and let it out slowly. "The lady is Emilie . . . de Sarron."

Gilbert and Vincent exchanged curious looks until dawning changed their expressions to mouth-gaping astonishment.

"You fucked *Emilie Embers*?" Gilbert exclaimed.

Fury rocked Joseph. He grabbed a fistful of Gilbert's justacorps and yanked him forward. Their noses butted. "If you ever—*ever*—call her that again—or anything similar—you will rue the day, brother," he hissed out through clenched teeth.

Gilbert's dark brows rose. "All right. I'm sorry, Joseph . . . It . . . It's just a shock . . . That you'd bed someone who has . . . er . . . who hasn't been seen in years." He quickly corrected himself.

Joseph released him.

Gilbert had the good grace to look contrite.

"Let me see if I understand this." Vincent rubbed the back of his neck. "You had a woman no one has seen in a decade, who you knew was both a virgin and Emilie de Sarron. And you used my name. *Why?*"

"Because she doesn't much care for Joseph. And I don't blame her. If I were her, I wouldn't either," Joseph explained. "Neither of you were at that party that night at the Marquis de Sere's château. Sere and his wife raised Emilie. Since their daughter was of similar age, they were both introduced to society that night. It was a grand affair. One that eventually garnered the Marquis's daughter her future husband. It turned out wonderfully for her and disastrously for Emilie." Joseph raked a hand through his hair. As always, whenever he thought about that night, his heart and stomach clenched.

"Augustin and Henri were well into their cups when the nasty commentary began," he continued, his tone sharper. "Comments about Emilie's likelihood of finding a husband. About her always wearing cloaks. Comments that drew a crowd around her and those two fools." Joseph shook his head. "I'd had my share of merrymaking and drink. I'd laughed along with the others around her at some of the things Augustin said. In my brandy-soaked mind, I actually thought Augustin's comments were to her benefit. That maybe the laughter and comments would cause her to finally cease wearing the unflattering garb. I behaved like a colossal ass. She kept looking at me, glancing my way. She knew a word from me would have silenced Augustin, Henri, and the crowd. I did nothing."

Those three words were as bitter as bile on his tongue. "That party changed everything for her," he said. "She'd finally had enough—and withdrew from everything and everyone. After having to tolerate names like Emilie Embers and worse all her life, who can fault her? She never deserved the pain she suffered."

"And you're making amends by lying to her and—despite being the last man she'd ever want, aside from Augustin and Henri—by claiming her maidenhead." It was Gilbert's turn to shake his head. "She isn't going to be very happy if she ever learns the truth."

No, she wouldn't be. She'd be deeply hurt. "That's why we're going to make certain she never learns the truth," Joseph countered, though he couldn't ignore the sharp pang of regret that stabbed into him. She'd cried out Vincent's name twice last night in ecstasy.

Joseph didn't know how much more of that he could take.

For the first time in his life, he was caught in his own web of lies. He couldn't stop wanting her. Couldn't get her forgiveness. Couldn't find peace without it.

"Joseph is making amends—in his own way. He's pleasuring the lady." Vincent turned to him. "You are pleasuring the lady, aren't you? I do have a reputation to uphold, you know."

By the mischief in his twin's eyes, Joseph knew Vincent was trying to leaven the moment. And he loved him for it.

Gilbert threw up his hands. "All right. I must know. You're going to get angry, Joseph, but I simply must ask. It's driving me mad . . . her scars. Everyone has heard rumors about how disfigured she is. How badly is she injured?"

A smile tugged hard at the corners of Joseph's mouth. There was nothing wrong with Emilie. It was time his brothers knew that. Joseph moved between his two brothers, hooked his arms around their necks, and drew their heads closer to him.

"I've seen nothing but the softest, most perfect, lavender-scented skin."

"Really? You have?" Gilbert asked.

"I have. Her body is lovely, and so sensitive to my touch, Gilbert, I can melt her with the lightest caress."

"*Oh?*" Intrigue and excitement tinged Gilbert's tone. He was affecting him.

Joseph hid his amusement. "And you'll appreciate this, Gilbert, knowing how much you love women's breasts . . . Hers are perfect."

"Perfect?" Gilbert asked.

"Perfect. She has the most beautiful tits you've ever seen. Unmarred, soft plump mounds with delicious pink nipples, made for a man's mouth. The tastiest teats, a man can't help but savor . . ."

Gilbert shifted. "Th-They're that good?"

"Oh, yes. That good. And then there's the blinding pleasure of being inside an untried, passionate woman, like Emilie. All that snug silky heat squeezing you so tightly, it makes you throb."

Vincent cleared his throat. "Th-Throb? Really?"

"Yes, really. You never want to leave her honeyed sheath. The torture is sublime. One that you want to go on," he said to Vincent, then turned to Gilbert, "and on . . . "

Smiling smugly, Joseph removed his arms from around his brothers and walked away, knowing he'd accomplished what he'd intended.

"*Merde*, Joseph." Gilbert adjusted his stiff cock in his breeches.

Vincent shook his head, his prick just as stirred. "You did that on purpose."

Joseph grinned. "An eye for an eye—for playing me earlier. And every word about how beyond perfect Emilie is, is absolutely true." Talking about Emilie hadn't been without a personal price. It had served to heighten his hunger. Hot excitement was rushing through his veins straight to his already engorged sex. "Now then, your clothes," he said to his twin. Taking off his knee-length coat, he tossed it onto a nearby chair. "I have a beautiful woman waiting for me—whom I'm most anxious to enjoy."

He wished it was no more than lust motivating his eagerness to see her. But there was an undercurrent of softer sentiment beneath the raw need.

One he hadn't yet mastered. Or quieted.

CHAPTER SEVEN

Emilie waited. And wondered.

Uneasy.

She could make no sense of the kiss Vincent had given her. Crowds funneled through the corridor in both directions and she was growing impatient for him to return.

Something was amiss. She wanted to know what. She had questions and wanted answers.

Glancing down the hall, she spotted him approaching through the throng. Or at least she thought it was him. He had on Vincent's clothing but Joseph's dark blue demi-mask.

It only added to her disquiet.

"Vincent, why are you wearing Joseph's mask?" she asked the moment he neared.

He halted his advance, touched the mask, and shrugged. "I must have picked up the wrong one after speaking to him."

It was the last thing he said before he shoved her hard against the wall and crushed his mouth to hers, snatching her breath from her lungs, his tongue possessing her mouth on her gasp. Her face trapped between his strong palms, he kissed her with dizzying intensity. Every nerve ending in her body leapt to life.

This was *it* . . .

The bud between her legs began to pulse, her questions dissolving as delicious raw hunger swamped her senses.

She laced her arms around his neck and held on to him during the maelstrom he caused with his powerful fiery kiss. Her nipples hardened and pressed against the inside of her chemise, eager for the carnal care he would bestow on them. She loved it when he touched them, what he did to them. What he did to her. She felt out of control, consumed by the yearning for him to fill that needy void between her legs. To feel that delicious stretching of her private muscles—bordering between pain and pleasure—as he fed her every delectable inch of his thick solid length.

"I need to fuck you," he growled against her mouth. His blunt statement practically buckling her knees. "I need to fuck you right *now*." In the hallway, with crowds of people moving about, he lifted her up against the wall, her toes barely touching the floor. She clung to his mouth, unwilling to relinquish it. She didn't care about anything except feeding her starved senses—with the only man who knew how to. He rolled his hips, pressing his solid shaft against her throbbing clit with the perfect pressure. Her cry was muffled against his lips.

"You have one moment, possibly two, to tell me whether you want me to take you right here or in private. Choose!" he rasped, and lowered her back down onto her feet, purposely brushing her sensitized clit down the bulge in his breeches. She lost her breath, the sensation stunning, despite the clothing between.

He had her mouth again, the heat and hunger of each kiss intoxicating her, inciting her further, obliterating everything but his mouth. His body. Him. His enlarged sex was up against her belly holding her focus, making her sex ache and leak.

Vincent tugged at her bodice, undressing her. She felt it loosen. Suddenly sounds around her rushed into her ears.

Her eyes snapped open and she saw that some people had stopped and were watching from across the corridor. It unsettled her down to the marrow.

She pulled her mouth away and grasped Vincent's hands, stilling them, her breathing quick and shallow.

"Private," she said in earnest.

His eyes were darkened with desire, his breathing as rapid as hers. "Pardon?"

"In private." She glanced over at those observing them from across the hall.

Vincent followed her gaze, tossing a look over his shoulder.

"Forget them." He pulled his hands free from her grasp, dipped his head, and reclaimed her mouth. His clever fingers were at her bodice once more.

Old insecurities rushed in on her. And a ten-year-old memory loomed—one where she'd been the center of attention in the crowd. One that threatened the wonderful sexual excitement she felt. Emilie may have found the courage to reveal some of her body to Vincent, but she couldn't do this in front of spectators.

She pulled back once more. "I can't." Not with those people watching.

He smiled. "*Ma belle*, you're at one of the Comtesse's gatherings. People do what they want wherever they want."

"I can't," was all she could say, a lump starting to form in her throat.

Thankfully he didn't argue or ask her to elaborate but simply took her hand and pressed a kiss to it. "Come with me."

Vincent led her through the throng in the hallway, away from the *voyeurs* who instantly protested their leaving, and through the crowded Grand Salon, passing a number of couples engaged in heavy copulation. Some against walls, others in chairs and on various other items of furniture. Chatter, laughter, and sounds of pleasure filled the air.

Vincent pushed open the doors leading to the gardens.

The night air was fresh and warm. Emilie filled her lungs with it as she rushed along, trying to keep up with his purposeful strides.

He'd cut a sharp right, walking along the perimeter of the château away from the groupings of people in the gardens. He didn't stop until he'd rounded the corner of the grand abode.

The moonlight hardly reached this side of her aunt's home. It was darker and secluded by the row of shrubs and bushes they'd slipped through.

Vincent ripped off his mask and tossed it to the grass, a smile on his seductive mouth. He pulled his justacorps off his strong shoulders and tossed that to the ground as well.

A fresh wave of arousal flooded her body.

"You're not wearing your cloak, Emilie. That pleases me." His long skillful fingers were undoing his vest.

She pulled off her mask and wig and threw them to the ground, her eyes fixed on the masculine perfection before her— slowly disrobing.

He tossed off his vest and hooked his thumbs in the waist-band of his breeches, his linen shirt still on.

"Are you wearing your caleçons?" The darkly seductive quality to his voice made her shiver.

"Perhaps."

He lifted a brow. "*Perhaps?* You'd better not be wearing your caleçons, Emilie. Or I'm going to have at that pert little derrière of yours before I have at your sweet sex."

A thrill tickled down her spine. That sounded more appealing than deterring.

He took a step toward her. She took a playful step back, keenly aware of the slickness between her legs. She loved how he made her heart race and her blood warm. Everything he said, every look he gave her, made her feel wild and wicked. And beautiful. It was almost inconceivable. His effect on her was so potent, she wondered if she could ever satisfy her desire for this man with just one lifetime.

"Lift up your skirts and show me whether or not you have your drawers on," he said.

She felt so wonderful it was difficult to keep a straight face. "That's an order. And as I've said before, I don't take orders."

He bolted for her. She squeaked in surprise, grabbed her train, and ran. Vincent caught her around the waist in short or-der, and brought her down with him onto the soft grass.

The next thing she knew, he had both her wrists in one strong hand pinned to the ground above her head, his body half covering hers.

Staring up at his handsome face, she panted, not from the exertion of her run, but from his tantalizing proximity.

He smiled, and with his other hand grabbed a fistful of her skirts. "Now we're going to see if you've been a good girl or a bad girl, Emilie." Slowly, he dragged her skirts up her legs, the fabrics lightly brushing against her bare skin. When he'd pulled them to her hips, his smile broadened. "Ah now, there's a pretty sight. No caleçons. Just soft blond curls . . . so very wet with your juices." He cupped her.

Softly, she moaned, spread her legs a little farther, and arched into his warm palm.

"You want me to take you, don't you, Emilie?" he said, caressing her sex with rhythmic strokes, but maddening they never reached as far as her throbbing bud.

"Oh, yes . . ."

She wiggled and arced, desperate for friction against her clit. With her wrists firmly pinned above her head, and his leg securely over hers, her movements were limited.

"I love it when you squirm," he said. "It's an arousing sight to behold, *ma belle*."

He lightly flicked her clit, then returned to his previous long luscious caresses over her erogenous flesh. Her frustration erupted from her throat. She writhed and twisted, still trying to rub against his elusive palm.

He chuckled. "You want your clit rubbed, Emilie?"

"Yes!" Dear God, she was dying for it. He was driving her to the brink of insanity.

"Well, you have been very good . . . no cloak . . . no caleçons. I suppose I should reward you."

"Good. Open your breeches and give me my reward."

He laughed. Then lowered his head and whispered in her ear, "That sounded like an order. I should tell you, I don't take orders."

He thrust three fingers into her. She cried out, the sharp pleasure in her sheath quivering up to the tips of her breasts.

"I haven't been able to stop thinking about this perfect snug sex." He pumped his fingers in and out, each stroke sublime. "As eager as I am to ride you, I'm going to taste you first."

He pulled his fingers out. She whimpered at the loss.

Holding her gaze, he drew his slick fingers across her bottom lip, applying her essence to it. Stunning her. Before she could react, he lowered his head and licked the juices off, then crushed his mouth to hers and drove his tongue inside. He kissed her hungry and hard. She tasted herself and him in her mouth, his intensity making her head spin.

His hand was at her bodice, finishing the job he'd commenced in the corridor. Pulling and tugging with practiced haste until he'd opened her bodice. Then his hand and mouth were gone. She opened her eyes to find him kneeling between her legs, pressing his palms against the grass on either side of her head. "I'm going to remove the gown and the stays."

Alarm shot through her.

He must have seen it. He brought his mouth down onto hers, his hand slipping inside her bodice, where he found her raised nipple and pinched it through her chemise. She mewed into his mouth, his perfect twists and tugs spiking her fever.

He broke the kiss. "You want more pleasure, don't you, Emilie?"

She closed her eyes and let her head loll to one side, the sensations at her breast echoing in her clit. "Yes."

"The sooner we remove the gown and stays, the sooner that will happen." He pinched the nipple, drawing a soft cry from her throat. "I'm going to make you come with my mouth. Then again with my cock." Holding her nipple captive, he pulled her chemise down, tucked it under her other breast, and drew the excited tip into his hot mouth. The voluptuous sensations streaked from her breast down to her aching core. Her sex responded with a warm gush.

She was trembling with need, with uncertainty, her mind awhirl.

"*Dieu.* Every part of you tastes so good." He released her breasts and gazed into her eyes. "I'll leave you in your chemise, but this night the gown and the rest go. What say you, Emilie?"

"I . . . I don't think—"

He pressed his fingers against her lips, silencing her. "You don't have to think . . . All you have to do is lie there just as you are, on your back, and enjoy," he said, removing his fingers from her lips. "What say you, *ma belle?* The chemise remains. Will you let me remove the rest?" He cupped her breast and gently grazed his thumb across it. "Say yes . . ."

If she stayed on her back, he wouldn't have access to the ugly marring.

She swallowed, her desperation to have him giving her the fortitude to push the word off her tongue. "*Yes.*"

His pleasure at her response showed on his face. Vincent wasted no time removing her gown, pulling the article off with her aid and very little trouble, and tossing it aside.

"If it's ruined, I'll buy you ten more," he said, attacking her stays and discarding them with as much ease. He tucked the loosened neckline of her chemise under her breasts and pushed the hem up to her navel, then sat back on his heels.

His gaze moved over her body, slowly taking in every inch of her.

"Ah, Emilie . . . you are so very beautiful," he marveled.

Emotions tightened her throat. She couldn't respond. She was grateful for whatever miracle brought this man to her.

He spread her folds and lightly scored his thumbs up and down her slick sex. "You look utterly delicious. A treat no man would pass up." He lowered himself and nestled between her thighs.

Emilie braced for the thrill of his mouth.

Warm lips pressed against her inner thigh. She flinched on contact. He trailed light bites and hot kisses toward her sex, getting closer and closer. Her pulse racing, she knew what he was about. This was something she'd told him she wanted in one of her letters. Had asked several questions about it after learning of it in one of her books, but never—ever—had she actually imagined it happening—with *him*.

He lowered his mouth onto her and gave her a soft luscious lick from her opening up to her throbbing bud, sending her arching off the grass with a cry.

"Emilie—" He reached up and toyed with her nipple until she focused her eyes on him. Her breathing was labored. "As much as I like your heated reactions, and they are delicious, *ma belle*, you're going to stay very still for me and let me savor you."

"Savor quickly."

Amusement entered his eyes, despite the clear desire reflecting back at her. "Was that an order, Emilie, because I don't take—"

"Please . . ." she quickly added. Damn him. He was toying with her when she was on the verge of expiring on the spot with lust.

"A plea for pleasure . . . That I can't deny." He lowered his dark head, eased his tongue inside her, and slowly drew it out. Sucking her. Kissing her. Licking her. The light sensations over her ultrasensitive sex making her whimper. She fought not to squirm, not wanting to give him any reason to stop.

He licked around her clit. She fisted the grass and squeezed her eyes shut, sensing his next move. Waiting for it. Desperate for it. Her legs trembled near his shoulders.

He closed his mouth over her engorged bud. She bit back her wail of delight; her body jerked as he gave her soft steady sucks. Each pull of his mouth melted her mind. She was racing closer and closer to a powerful orgasm. Unstoppable. Barreling toward her. Then he lightly bit her.

Ecstasy exploded inside. She drove her hips up hard against his mouth, pleasure flooding her senses, her sex contracting in rhythm with her wild heart.

He continued to lap at her sex, her juices, cherishing her private flesh with an unfed hunger. Tirelessly enjoying her until she quieted, boneless, her legs leaden and sprawled apart.

She didn't care if she was lying on the grass, exposed to him. She felt no shame. Just an overwhelming sense of bliss.

Vincent rose to his feet between her legs. Holding her gaze, he wiped his chin with the back of his hand, and licked his bottom lip clean of her essence.

"I love the way you taste," he said with such raw hunger in his eyes, it sent a quiver through her womb. A surprising reaction given the magnitude of her climax.

She watched him strip off the remainder of his clothing, luxuriating in his strong chest, his rippled abdomen, her gaze moving all the way down to his large cock. It held her attention as he knelt down between her knees. Memories of his talents with that particular part of his male anatomy swirled though her system.

She sat up and reached for his shaft. Wrapping her fingers around its base, she stroked his sex up to the crest of his cock and back down—in the very way he'd described in his letter when she'd asked where and how men liked to be touched. He briefly closed his eyes.

"I want to taste you, Vincent." She felt him tense.

Gently, he pulled her hand away from his prick and leaned into her, forcing her onto her back once more, and lowered himself on top of her. "Two things, *Emilie*. First, I don't like the name 'Vincent' much. I don't want to hear it during sex."

Before she could comment on his rather absurd statement, he stroked his cock along her wet folds, and grazed her clit, making her gasp.

"Second," he continued. "As much as I'd love to have my cock in that beautiful mouth—and I most definitely will next time—I have to get back inside that slick tight sheath of yours. Now." He lodged himself at her entrance and pushed.

She lost her breath the moment the crest of his shaft slipped inside her. A groan rumbled out of his chest, and reverberated through her. He bore down on her, deliciously forcing her sex to stretch as he fed her his length a glorious inch at a time. His slow and steady possession incited a fresh, fierce hunger.

"*Christ,* I love how you're even tighter after an orgasm." His voice was hoarse.

He withdrew, and just as he was sliding back in, she became impatient and jerked her hips upward, forcing the head of his cock to collide with her womb, making them both gasp.

He growled her name and buried his face in her hair, his labored breaths matching her own, warming her neck. Softly he said, "You feel so good . . . I'm throbbing so hard."

So was she. Her feminine walls pulsed around his large thick cock.

Lightly, he bit her earlobe then the sensitive spot under her ear. "Lovely Princess Emilie, you are an enchantress . . . and more heaven than any mortal man has the right to." He began to slide in and out of her.

She laced her arms around him.

She didn't know how he did it, but his words were like a balm. Taking away years of pain. Transforming her. Had any other man uttered those words, she would have dismissed them, convinced he was mocking her. But from Vincent's mouth, he made her believe the unbelievable.

Because she trusted him.

Because she loved him.

She sought out his mouth and kissed him with a mix of love and lust. Pulling her arms from around his neck, he pinned her wrists to the ground, picking up the pace, giving her deep solid thrusts. Pinned under him, all she could do was take each one, sensations radiating out from her core to her entire body in dazzling waves with each downstroke. She reveled in every plunge and drag as he rammed her with unbridled abandon. Violently aroused, she was swept up in the stunning sensations flooding her system.

Light pulsing inside her sex signaled the beginnings of her climax. She strained against him, trembling on the edge. "I'm going to . . ."

Her orgasm slammed into her, ripping a scream from her throat, sending violent spasms through her core and around this thrusting cock.

He growled and grunted, driving into her unrelenting, until the spasms began to ebb. Then he jerked his cock out, crushed her to him, and groaned long and hard against her neck. His body shuddered, his muscles tense and taut as he spent himself on the grass between her legs.

Languid, Emilie caressed his back, holding him until his body relaxed and his breathing slowed.

Lifting his head, he gazed down at her. His blue eyes were soft, his smile moving her to one as well.

"I loved that," he said.

I love you . . . She caressed his cheek. "Me, too."

She couldn't reveal her feelings any more than she could reveal her scars. There were some walls she just couldn't scale. Despite the recent changes in her, she couldn't lay herself that bare. She hadn't survived this long by exposing herself completely. No doubt if she did, he'd run.

Holding her tightly, Joseph rolled, pulling her on top. She tensed. Smiling, he slipped his hand behind her head and pulled her mouth to his, kissing her sweet lips. He felt so good, his blood humming in his veins. All because of his one and only Emilie. Skimming his free hand under her chemise, he followed the lush curve of her bottom upward until he touched upon a rough, thick, bumpy skin.

She shrieked against his mouth and jumped away so quickly it stunned him.

He snapped open his eyes to find her sitting several feet away, looking positively stricken and ready to bolt.

"You said you wouldn't!" Her beautiful eyes were full of hurt and panic.

Merde. If his brain hadn't been so foggy in the afterglow of a powerful orgasm, he wouldn't have made the blunder.

Joseph raised himself up onto one elbow. "I'm sorry, Emilie. I wasn't trying to remove the chemise. I like touching you. I got carried away. I didn't mean to upset you."

"I've got to go." She dropped to her knees and was about to stand.

"Wait!" He sat up. "Don't go. Come here, *ma belle.*" He patted the spot beside him. "On your back, beside me." He reclined back onto his side. "The night is young still. Stay with me." Joseph held out his hand.

Silently he beseeched her.

She looked unsure and he hated seeing the mistrust in her eyes. It gored him in the heart.

"It won't happen again. I promise." Seeing the look on her face made him realize just what a daunting task it was going to be to have her discard the chemise. One that he was even more determined to take on. But it required a gentle hand. And a good deal of patience and understanding.

She rose. He held his breath.

Emilie walked over and lay down beside him. Joseph wanted to shout with joy.

She snuggled closer. "Never again," she warned.

He leaned over and lightly kissed her. "Emilie, I'm certain it's not as bad as you believe."

She stiffened. "It's very bad."

"Why not let me be the judge?"

"No! It would ruin everything between us." She lifted her head and tried to sit up, but he quickly claimed her mouth and eased her back down. Capturing her sweet face, he gave her a long unhurried kiss, cherishing her mouth, her taste, his tongue giving hers slow, swirling caresses.

When at last he ended the kiss, her body was no longer rigid, but soft and wonderfully yielding. She gazed up at him with such touching tenderness in her eyes, the sight of which filled his heart with a deep sense of contentment.

"I didn't mean to get so upset with you, Vincent. I'm sorry."

"No need to apologize. I understand. It was entirely my fault."

A smile formed on her lovely mouth. "I'm so glad you're nothing like your brother."

Joseph's chest tightened. He hated the low opinion she had of him. Her disregard for him, though not unfounded, bothered him to the core of his being. "You know," he said, brushing an errant blond curl off her cheek, "Joseph is sorry for what he did or rather what he didn't do that night. He told me so himself."

Still smiling, she rose up onto her elbow, matching his pose. "No he didn't, Vincent. But I do adore you for wanting to offer an apology on his behalf. The mighty Joseph d'Alumbert would never admit to any wrongdoing against anyone."

She was right. He never would. Never had. Until tonight when his brothers had managed to do something rare—corner him.

"Men like Joseph don't change."

That was just the thing. He had changed. He hadn't wanted it, hadn't expected it, but it had happened. And it was all because of one flaxen-haired beauty—a woman who stirred soft sentiment during sex and all the time in between.

CHAPTER EIGHT

Joseph put on his gray justacorps and secured his black demi-mask. It was midafternoon and he was anxious to see Emilie.

He still hadn't coaxed her out of the final article of clothing—her chemise. Still hadn't managed to convince her to let him stay the night, that she shouldn't worry if in her sleep he caught a glimpse of her scars.

Yet despite his failings, over the last four days they'd shared in the most soul-satisfying sex. It was the greatest bliss he'd ever known. Not to mention he'd taken her in every position she favored in her naughty book. At least twice.

She was the first person he sought out upon awakening and the last person he saw before retiring for bed—usually in the early hours of dawn. He'd taken up eating supper in the grand dining hall by her side—away from his brothers and friends, his brothers making a point to walk by every night to bid *"Vincent"*—stressing the name between chuckles—a *bon appetite*.

Joseph smoothed his vest and smiled. Emilie had told him she'd be wearing a very special costume this night. He couldn't wait to see it. Couldn't wait to take her out of it.

She'd looked comely in anything. Even barefoot wearing sackcloth.

He snatched open the door and was surprised to find a solemn-looking servant, a much older man, standing at his door ready to knock.

"My lord."

"Yes. What is it?" Instantly irked, he wanted no delays in seeing Emilie.

"Madame de Naylon, Comtesse de Saint-Arnaud, wishes to speak to you."

His hostess?

"Can this wait? I'm rather busy."

"She insists you join her immediately in the library. Please follow me."

The elderly man gave a short bow and, turning on a heel, made his way down the hall.

Merde. What on earth could Emilie's aunt want?

*****

The Comtesse de Saint-Arnaud rose from behind her desk the moment Joseph entered the library.

The servant closed the doors behind him.

Joseph pulled off his mask. "Madame, you wished to see me?"

She walked around the desk in silence and stopped before him. "I presume I'm speaking with the Marquis de Valle, Joseph d'Alumbert?"

"You are."

"Good, then let me be plain and to the point."

"I'd appreciate that, madame. What is this about?"

"My niece. I believe you are toying with her."

Joseph's heart gave a small lurch. He schooled his features, affecting a look of indifference. "Possibly. The ladies are wearing masks. I couldn't say exactly who I'm 'toying with.' Isn't that the point to your gatherings? Anonymity?"

"Don't try to be clever. My niece is very dear to me. Her experience with men has been sadly limited. She believes she's having an affair with Vincent d'Alumbert."

"Then you should speak with him." Joseph turned to leave.

"He has a scar on his shoulder, doesn't he?" the Comtesse called out.

That stopped Joseph dead in his tracks. He faced the older woman once more. "Pardon?"

"You heard me well enough. Apparently there aren't many ways to tell the two of you apart. But according to your very good friend, Augustin de Coix, who was well into his cups earlier, as boys he and Vincent climbed a tree. Vincent fell out and suffered a rather nasty gash to his shoulder. It left quite the mark apparently. What do you suppose my niece will answer if I ask her whether her lover has any markings on his shoulder?"

Joseph's stomach dropped. "I don't know which niece you speak of, since it is my understanding you have more than one. However, if my brother is truly fucking her, her answer will be, 'No.' I was the one who fell out of the tree. Not Vincent," he lied. "Augustin is a fool who can't recall what he did yesterday, much less an incident that occurred many years ago."

"You'll show me your scar, of course."

Joseph walked up to the Comtesse. "Madame, I suggest you remember whom you are speaking to. I'm going to ignore the insulting request you've just made. I'm going to pretend this conversation never happened, for your sake."

He marched out.

Merde. He had to find Vincent. He had to change clothes with him.

He had to speak to him. Fast.

*****

Emilie walked along the corridor that led to the grand dining hall. Her gown was white with tiny pearls embellishing the bodice. On her demi-mask, there were more pearls and soft white plumes. The square neckline was adorned with the finest sheerest gauze. She felt beautiful in her costume.

As beautiful and elegant as a swan. And that was exactly what she'd chosen as her masquerade attire this eve. A swan. She hadn't even bothered with a wig. She felt so changed, she was certain no one would recognize her.

She couldn't wait to see Vincent. Couldn't wait to see his reaction to her lovely costume.

Just then she spotted him stepping out of the library. He was wearing exactly what he said he'd wear—a black demi-mask and gray justacorps and breeches.

Rushing through the crowd, she walked right up to him, beaming. "Vincent."

He looked startled to see her, then he glanced over his shoulder. Her aunt stood in the doorway of the library, closely observing them.

"You have me mistaken for my brother," he said and stepped around her.

She laughed and caught his hand, hauling his progress. "Vincent, what game are you playing?" She stepped in close and lightly ran her finger along the side of his neck. "You sport the love bite I gave you last night."

"Good evening, *Vincent*," his twin said, grinning as he approached with the youngest d'Alumbert, Gilbert.

Vincent lowered his head and squeezed her hand. She heard a very clear *"Merde"* slip past his lips.

"Good sirs, will you kindly step into the library," Pauline said to the three Alumberts before Emilie. "Darling, you come, too." Her aunt was looking straight at her.

Emilie was seized by an uneasy feeling. One she couldn't shake as she entered the room with the Duc de Vernant's three sons.

Joseph continued to hold Emilie's hand, refusing to let it go just yet. Knowing his lies were about to be revealed, he wanted her touch until the moment she'd likely rip it away from him.

"Do you have anything to say, Monsieur Joseph d'Alumbert?" the Comtesse said.

"Indeed I do," Vincent responded for him. "I'd like to know why I'm in here. There are festivities I'm missing out on."

Madame de Saint-Arnaud let out a sigh, clearly exasperated. "I'm speaking to Joseph d'Alumbert." She looked straight at him.

Vincent responded, "And I'm answering. I am Joseph."

"Are you still going to try to deceive her?" Madame de Saint-Arnaud asked Joseph pointedly, ignoring Vincent.

Joseph couldn't voice the words. He simply held Emilie's hand, his thumb gently caressing it. His heart hurt so keenly, as if it were tearing in two.

"What is happening?" Emilie spoke, her soft green eyes on him.

Gilbert strolled up to the Comtesse, smiling. "Dear Madame de Saint-Arnaud, you are clearly confused. But don't be embarrassed by it. They look so much alike, that I, their own brother, sometimes confuse them. A common mistake. Now, why don't we put our masks back on and enjoy the rest of the evening. What say you?" He spoke to the group before him.

"I say that this man"—the Comtesse pointed straight at Joseph—"just entered this very room moments ago and admitted to me he was Joseph d'Alumbert."

"Did you do that?" Emilie asked him, but before Joseph could respond, Vincent interjected with a laugh.

"Vincent does that all the time." Vincent shook his head. "He envies me, you see. I am, after all, the firstborn. The heir. Pay him no mind."

"Forget it, Vincent." At last he found his voice, simply because the lies had become too much to bear. Joseph looked at Emilie, cherishing the last moments her soft delicate hand rested in his. "I am Joseph. He is Vincent, a good brother, and a poor liar."

"Really? I thought I was a good liar."

"And I am Gilbert d'Alumbert." Smiling, Gilbert walked up to Emilie and gave a short bow. "Apparently, I'm the only one who hasn't kissed you, but I'm happy to accommodate—"

"You're not helping," Joseph cut him off sharply. This was no time for his brothers' usual foolery.

Her sweet lips parted, she stepped in front of him, her hand still absently in his, her eyes moving from Vincent back to him. She was a vision in her white gown. He hated it that he couldn't pull her to him. He hated the distress etched on her brow, her breasts rising and falling with her quickened breaths.

"The only one who hasn't kissed me?" she said softly. Incredulous. Shocked.

"Good Lord, you haven't shared her without her knowledge, have you? I've heard that you gentlemen have been known to do that, but—"

"No!" Joseph quickly silenced the Comtesse's rant. He squeezed Emilie's hand to gain her full attention. "It wasn't like that. You've been with me. Just me. Joseph."

"Except our kiss in the hallway . . . Which was quite delicious indeed," Vincent said. "I've never touched you."

"*Merde*, Vincent. That's not helpful," Joseph exploded.

Vincent held up his hands. "Sorry, Joseph."

Emilie pulled her hand from his grip. Tears glistened in her eyes. "This is all a game to you, isn't it? A cruel game."

"No, this is no game. The letters, what happened between us here, were real. Sincere." Joseph caressed her cheek. She jumped back.

"Don't touch me, Joseph."

Those words sliced him deeply.

"Do not speak to me about sincerity when you've done nothing but deceive me! What are you going to do now?" she asked him. "Run about and tell all your friends how you had Singed Emilie de Sarron?" She angrily swiped a tear that ran down her cheek. "Just think of all the laughs you will have. We all know how much you love to laugh at another's expense."

She turned and walked out of the room.

Joseph felt as if the air had been knocked out of his lungs. He placed his hands on his hips, trying to breathe.

"I hope you're pleased with yourself," the Comtesse said.

Joseph's gaze shot up to hers. Teeth clenched, he growled, "Madame, if you were a man, I'd lay you low for what you've just done."

"What I've just done? Sir, you blame me for your poor conduct?"

The commotion outside grabbed Joseph's attention. There was laughter. And he could hear Augustin's booming voice.

Joseph stalked from the room. Entering the hallway, he noticed a crowd had formed in the grand vestibule. He gravitated to it. His heart missed a beat when he saw Emilie in the middle of the crowd with Augustin beside her.

He was laughing along with the throng. Emilie was unmasked; the beautiful swan's mask lay on the floor.

She cracked her palm against Augustin's cheek. "You are vile and a fool."

The crowd roared.

Joseph pushed his way through the mass and entered the center.

Augustin rubbed his cheek, no longer looking as amused as before. "Ah, Joseph!" He pointed to Emilie. "Look who has been at the gathering. Some of the men may have actually fucked Singed de Sarron."

Joseph smashed his fist against Augustin's thick jaw, knocking the man to the floor. A gasp rippled in the crowd. Taking in a deep breath, he let it out slowly, then calmly clasped his hands behind his back. Slowly, he strolled the perimeter of the large circle the throng had created around him, Emilie and Augustin, gazing out at the many faces within the mass. "None of the men here have had this woman. None of you have been that fortunate. But I have—Joseph of the House of Alumbert, heir of the Duc de Vernant. Anyone who finds amusement in that may step into the circle. I promise you, if you do, you will be joining the Comte de Coix on the floor."

He paused and took in the dead silence.

Joseph continued. "Let me correct everyone on her name. You may call her Mademoiselle de Sarron. Or if she permits it, Emilie. But I have different names for her."

Joseph stopped and faced her. Her gaze nervously darted to the crowd, and back to him.

"She is Emilie the Brave. Emilie the Beautiful. Emilie Who-Makes-Me-Laugh. Emilie Who-Gives-Me-Joy. Emilie Who-

Has-Stolen-My-Heart de Sarron. And I want her to be mine for the rest of my life, more than words can say . . ."

Another collective gasp rose from the onlookers, but no one was as stunned as the blond beauty before him.

"Will you marry me?" he asked from the heart.

Her chin dropped and he saw the glistening paths of tears she was too proud to show.

"Out!" he commanded the crowd without removing his gaze from her. Reluctantly, people began to disperse, murmuring as they left.

Joseph approached her, cupped her face, and tilted her chin up. When her gaze met his, he gently wiped her tears with his thumbs. "I've wanted to tell you for the longest time how sorry I am about what happened that night. I've wished a thousand times that I'd done something—anything that would have spared you the pain of that eve. Initially I wrote to you a year ago out of guilt—a troubled conscience—but I fell in love with you a little more with each and every letter, and every moment that we've shared here. I'm sorry for the deceptions, but I won't apologize for being with you. I'm not sorry about that. There's a connection between us and it's wonderful. You know it, Emilie. You feel it, too. Say you'll marry me. I love you, Emilie, and I know you love me. I can see it in the way you look at me. I can feel it in the way you touch me. Be mine, *ma belle*."

Tears slid down her cheeks. She shook her head. "How can you want to marry me? You don't even know what I look like . . . what the scars look like."

He smiled tenderly at her. "I don't care."

"You say that because you've never seen them . . ."

"I say that because I've seen all I need to see to know unequivocally—you're what I want. Whom I love." Words tumbling from his mouth were flowing from his heart. Words that just felt so right.

She closed her eyes and swallowed hard. He took advantage of the moment, dipped his head, and kissed her. A soft gentle kiss, praying all the while she wouldn't push him away.

The moment he felt her return his kiss, her lips parting for him, he slid his tongue inside, reeling with jubilation. Tender yet passionate, it was filled with more emotion than any kiss he'd ever given or received.

It heated his blood and warmed his heart.

He needed her. They needed each other.

Impatient to have her, he broke the kiss and grabbed her hand. "Come with me."

Joseph briskly crossed the vestibule, climbed the stairs, and made it back to her private apartments in no time. The moment he closed her door, he pushed her up against it and feasted on her sweet mouth, his fingers immediately at the fastenings of her bodice, undoing them before she could protest.

But she didn't protest. She softly moaned into his mouth, her hands moving to his back, fisting his justacorps.

"Emilie . . . admit you love me. I can even feel it in your kiss. I'm the same man you corresponded with. Whom you wanted to share your most intimate thoughts and longings with. I'm the same man who's made love to you every night since your arrival. Your hurt and anger at me for my part in that night so long ago is not unjust. If I could change that night, I would. Let me make it up to you—by loving you, by cherishing you the rest of our lives. Say it, Emilie. Speak the truth. Say you love me. Say you'll marry me."

Emilie was trembling. It was the truth! She couldn't believe she was deeply in love with Joseph d'Alumbert. That she had been all this time. "I do love you. But I can't—"

He cut off her words with a brief, hard kiss, then he stepped back and removed his justacorps. Then his vest.

"What are you doing?"

"I'm going to have you. No gown, no stays, no chemise. Nothing between us."

"I can't do that. I can't expose myself that way."

"Yes you can, Emilie."

"No! It's—It's the reason I can't marry you. If you were to see how ugly the scars are, you'd understand. You'd be repulsed. And you wouldn't want me for a wife."

He smiled. "I could never be repulsed by you. But if you think you can drive me away with your scars, go ahead and try. It won't work." He opened his breeches and pulled off his linen shirt, discarding it. "Take your clothes off, Emilie." He took her hand and brought it to his cock. She couldn't stop herself from wrapping her fingers around his hard shaft. Arousal flared in her belly. He stroked her hand along his length. "I want you. Not just now. But forever. You're mine. I'm going to come inside you. I'm going to stay inside you until the end."

Her sex clenched hard and moistened. Every fiber of her being screamed, *Yes! Do it!*

Suddenly she was sick of hiding. Concealing. Afraid of her scars being seen. This was the man she'd shared so much with.

He said he couldn't be repelled. Could that miraculously be true?

She wanted to be with this man. She loved seeing herself through his eyes. She loved how happy she felt around him.

She loved him so very much. She wanted to hold on to the bliss he brought—for a lifetime. And her scars were the final obstacle in their path.

Emilie pulled her hand away from his beautiful prick and began to strip. A slow grin formed on his handsome face. He helped her discard her clothing down to the final chemise.

Her beautiful swan costume lay scattered on the floor.

He picked her up in his arms and carried her to her bedchambers. Setting her feet down before the bed, he removed the last of his clothing.

He stood naked, unabashed. "Your turn, Emilie."

Her heart pounding, she drew in a shaky breath. *I can do this.*

Grabbing handfuls of her chemise, she pulled it up over her head in one quick movement, fearing that with a slower progress she'd falter.

Standing naked, she met his gaze.

He was smiling. "I just see beauty."

That's because I haven't turned around and showed you my back yet. Emilie swallowed hard and forced herself to turn her back to him.

Facing him were her scars, covering her back, and down the backs of her arms to her elbows. Pink to dark red blotchy skin. Thick. And raised. And uneven.

And horrible to behold.

Not having the courage to turn back around to see his reaction, she waited for him to speak, her insides quaking.

She felt his lips against her shoulder first. She lurched. He slipped his arm around her waist and bent her forward. She braced her palms against the mattress. Kiss after kiss was pressed against her back as he slowly made his way down her spine. Tears welled in her eyes and fell onto the bed. She was so stunned, so moved, she couldn't believe what he was doing.

He straightened, leaned over her, and near her ear he repeated, "I just see beauty."

Shaking, she couldn't speak. Overwhelmed by emotion. Overwhelmed by him. Her only sounds were her ragged breaths.

He captured her nipple between his strong warm fingers and gave it luscious rolls and tugs, instantly swamping her with sensations. His other hand reached around and he began fingering her with devastating finesse. "I'm going to take you from behind—one of my favorite positions."

Already wet and feverish for him, she would have agreed to just about anything.

"You want my cock, Emilie?"

"Yes!"

"Yes, *Joseph*. I want to hear my name from your lips."

"*Joseph* . . . I want your . . . cock."

He slid his shaft along her slick folds, grazing the engorged head over her pulsing clit. She gasped.

"Joseph, I love you. Say it." He was smiling. She could hear it in his tone. The rhythmic strokes across her private flesh were sublime, flooding her body with pleasure, inciting an all-consuming hunger.

"Say it, Emilie," he insisted.

"I love you, Joseph."

"I will marry you, *Joseph*," he said.

"Yes! Yes, I will marry you, Joseph . . . Please . . . I want you inside me."

"There's a request I cannot refuse." Grabbing her hips firmly, he drove his cock into her.

She cried out and fisted the counterpane, deliciously stretched and full by his possession.

He thrust again. And again. Gliding his shaft over a sweet spot inside her slick walls, giving her a barrage of knee-weakening sensations. Making her moan and gasp.

"*Dieu*, I love your tight grip on me. How does it feel? You like being taken this way, don't you?"

"Yes!" She'd love anything as long as it was him doing the taking.

Pushing her bottom toward him, she was eager for more, reveling in the glorious friction of his driving sex. In the stunning depth of his every plunge. The pleasure was so keen, and she was fast approaching a shattering release.

"You're going to come, aren't you? I can feel it," he rasped. "You're clenching around me . . . with those mind-bending little spasms."

Dear God, it was true. She couldn't help it. Couldn't stop it. Her inner muscles were milking his shaft greedily, ravenous for more.

"Come with me, Emilie. I want you to come when I do."

Oh, how she wanted that.

He slipped his hand between her legs, paying homage to that tiny bud so sensitized with desire, sending torrents of scintillating sensations straight into her core. The strokes of his hand and the strokes of his sex were double the pleasure. And shot her into ecstasy, his roar of pleasure joining her scream as he pulsed inside her and poured himself into her depths.

She sobbed with joy and rapture, her sex wildly contracting around his plunging shaft, milking him until he'd spent his final drop.

Her breathing and her thundering heart slowed; her legs and arms were lax.

Emilie's entire body hummed with satisfaction. And bliss.

He swept her up in his arms and deposited her tenderly on the bed.

Lying beside her, he pulled her to him. "You're going to let me stay the night."

She smiled. "Is that an order?"

Joseph returned her smile. "Take it any way you wish. I'm not leaving."

"I know. That's why I love you." Slipping her hand behind his head, she pulled him to her for a kiss. She was lying completely naked and comfortable in his arms—loved and in love.

The transformation was complete.

By the magic of this man, Emilie de Sarron had indeed changed from an ugly duckling to a most beautiful swan.

HISTORICAL TIDBIT

If you've read my other Fiery Tales, you know that I enjoy sharing some of the interesting background research, and the real historical figures I use to help shape the characters and stories in this series. I love giving you a behind-the-scenes look into my books.

However, this time what shaped this story was a little bit of history—but mostly three contemporary incredible sisters I happen to see on TV.

You see, the idea for THE LOVELY DUCKLING came to me in Washington, D.C. while at the RWA conference. I had just landed my first contract with Penguin. I jumped on a plane, and flew down to meet my agent and editor in person for the first time.

I knew that while I was in Washington my editor wanted to discuss if I'd like to write more steamy, fairy tale inspired stories. My agent asked if I thought I could come up with three more fairy tales, set in a historical setting, and give them an interesting twist.

My answer—Heck, yes!

I've always loved *The Ugly Duckling.* I really wanted to do my own version of this wonderful tale. I tried to come up with different ways to make my heroine "ugly". Different things that would make her feel unattractive. I dismissed them all, one after another.

Then, in my hotel room, while I was getting ready for dinner, I had the TV on.

There was a news feature about three sisters—beautiful women—triplets. They were taking about the fire they were in as infants. A fire that had claimed their mother's life. These twenty-two year old women talked about how difficult it was growing up. The incessant teasing and horrible taunts they endured. How they always wore long-sleeved clothing—no matter the temperature—to cover up the scars on their bodies and arms.

I was moved by their courage. And by the two boyfriends two of these women were dating. By the end of the feature, I think I was a tad in love with them, too. One of the guys had been dating one of the triplets for two years and hadn't even seen her bare arms—until one hot summer night. That was the night he finally convinced her to remove her sweatshirt. (He knew she wore a t-shirt underneath and that she was uncomfortable, given the heat). As she explained to the reporter, she *finally* got the nerve to show him her scars. She said to him (with tears in her eyes), "Here I am. Take me or leave me!"

Her boyfriend is definitely hero material. He relayed to the reporter that his response, after taking in the deeply scarred skin was, "I'll take you."

Seriously, I was in tears myself. And that was the moment both Emilie de Sarron and Joseph d'Alumbert were born in my imagination.

As to the historical tidbits in this story, the salacious gathering depicted in this Fiery Tale were common in seventeenth century France. And as it happened to Emilie in THE LOVELY DUCKLING, so too were lawsuits over guardianship of a minor child with wealth. Families often fought for custody so that they would have control of the child's fortune until they came of age. Sadly, fighting over family money isn't a modern day concept.

The glittering court of Louis XIV wasn't just salacious and elegant. It was the very time period that the father of fairy tales,

Charles Perrault—author of *The Tales of Mother Goose*—wrote stories that have delighted generations: *Sleeping Beauty, Little Red Riding Hood, Puss in Boots* and *Cinderella* to name a few.

I hope you enjoyed your time in the opulent world when fairy tales were born. Please see the end for a delicious excerpt of yet another Fiery Tale!

Happy reading!

GLOSSARY

Antechamber   The sitting room in a lord's or lady's private apartments (chambers) within their hôtel or château.

Caleçons   Drawers/underwear.

Chambers   Another word for private apartments. A lord's or lady's chambers consisted of a bedroom, a sitting room, a bathroom, and a *cabinet* (office). Some chambers were bigger and more elaborate than others. Some *cabinets* were so large, they were used for private meetings.

Chère   Dear one. (French endearment for a woman, *cher* for a man).

Chérie   Darling or cherished one. (French endearment for a woman, *chéri* for a man).

Comte/Comtesse   Count/Countess.

Dieu   God.

Duc/Duchesse   Duke/Duchess.

Hôtel/Château   The upper class and the wealthy bourgeois (middle class) often had a city mansion in Paris (*hôtel*) in addition to their palatial country estate(s) (*château*).

Justacorps   A fitted knee-length coat, worn over a man's vest and breeches.

Merde   Shit.

Ma belle   My beauty. (French endearment for a woman).

Seigneur Dieu   Lord God.

READ AN EXCERPT OF
THE PRINCESS & THE DIAMONDS

Inspired by the tale of The Princess & the Pea, a hot historical romance novella from the acclaimed Fiery Tales series.

Princess Gabrielle can't sleep at night. There is something hard in her bed. No, not just the stolen diamonds tucked under her mattress, but the handsome Marquis on it....whose talent in the art of pleasure she can't resist. But he threatens her secret mission, and worse, she stands to lose far more than the diamonds—her heart is at stake....

Mathias is on a mission of his own. The last person he expected to find in an illegal gaming den was a mysterious beauty. The intensity of their attraction takes him off guard. And soon he realizes he may have found the only woman he can't get enough of...

***Originally published in
THE PRINCESS IN HIS BED anthology.

CHAPTER ONE

"Are you absolutely certain you want to do this, Montfort? You'll be turning on your peers," Renault de Sard asked from behind his desk.

Mathias Paul Thomas de Tesson, Marquis de Montfort, found himself seated in the home of the Lieutenant General of Police of Paris, sequestered in his private study—rather than at his public office.

This was no ordinary meeting. Its secrecy paramount. The mission at hand was to topple some of the highest-ranking nobles of the realm, aristocracy that considered themselves untouchable. Above the law.

Unfazed by the Lieutenant General's comment, Mathias sat back in the silk upholstered chair.

"You need a spy. The King wants his ban on Basset enforced. And I am at your disposal." He'd been eager since Sard approached him two days ago. In fact, this was the first time since Charles's death that he felt any fire at all. "Besides, you know as well as I do they turn on each other every time they sit at a Basset table." He couldn't keep the disdain from his tone. His disgust wasn't simply directed at those breaking the King's new law, but at himself.

He hadn't been any different than those who still gambled at the game. Lord knows he was no stranger to the gaming tables. Women and gambling had been his favorite forms of recreation.

He'd enjoyed vice. And with his wealth and skill, the monetary losses had been minimal and without detriment.

Gambling had never really cost him. Until five months ago. Five months ago Basset had cost him the life of his closest friend.

"Yes, well, I have finally impressed upon His Majesty that if we don't make examples of men of high rank, his edict will continue to be ignored—and more prominent families will be brought to their ruin," Sard said.

Mathias didn't need anyone to explain to him the damage Basset caused. The card game wildly popular among those wealthy enough to play with high stakes, Basset could make or break fortunes in minutes. He'd seen both men and women lose staggering sums.

Lose everything.

He'd stopped playing when the King had issued his decree. He only wished Charles had done the same. He'd be alive now. His wife wouldn't be a widow, and his young daughter would still have her father.

Charles would never have lost all that he owned—or committed suicide.

"I quite agree," Mathias said. "Unless you bring to heel those involved who are of the highest rank, the wealthy will continue to pay the King's edict no mind." He stretched out his legs and crossed his arms over his chest. "What do you wish me to do, and how soon may I begin?"

"I like your enthusiasm, Montfort." Sard smiled. "I need you to gather names. Tell me who the regular players are, who the biggest players are. And of course, most importantly, who the dealer is—the one that minds the bank—and reaps the biggest rewards at the game."

Mathias gave the Lieutenant of Police a mirthless smile. "No problem."

"Do you have anyone in particular in mind we can focus on? If we're to make an example of him, he must be highly notable."

Mathias's smile broadened. "I've the perfect man to suggest. The Duc de Navers. Is that notable enough for you, Sard?"

Sard lifted his brows. "A duc?" His brown eyes danced with delight. "Oh, Navers will do just fine. Perfectly, in fact."

It was perfect. In so many ways. Charles lost his wealth to Navers. In his very own mansion in the city—Hôtel de Navers— the Duc was making a fortune from his biweekly private gaming den. Right under the nose of the Paris police. Without concern. Or regard for the royal edict.

Navers wasn't the only noble who hosted Basset games. But he was the one Mathias wanted to focus on.

"Navers's games are masked," Mathias added. "Only those with funds enough to play are permitted. That includes any wealthy merchants from the bourgeois. The mask allows for anonymity, and makes everyone equal while playing Basset, regardless of title. Money is the only thing that is held in esteem at the gaming table. If you lose everything, then and only then are you unmasked. Before you're permitted to leave the table, you are made to sign your ruin."

At that Sard frowned. "How will you know who is who?"

"I've played many years with the same people. It won't be difficult for me to determine who is in attendance. Mannerisms, expressions of speech are not covered by a mask. Neither is a man's or woman's style of play. No one will go unreported."

"And you've no conflict of conscience or qualms in advising me of each and every person there?" Sard pressed. Clearly the man wanted to be assured of his commitment to the mission.

"None," he said without hesitation. "The rule in Basset is that you have no friends." He didn't have any friends left. At least none like Charles.

For him and his family, for others who'd suffered the same fate and for any further such tragedies, he was going to put an end to Basset once and for all.

Nothing and no one was going to stop him.

*****

"Is there anything I can say that will stop you from doing this?" Bernadette asked, worried.

"Or I?" Caroline looked just as concerned.

"No." Gabrielle's response was unequivocal as she studied her attire in the mirror with a critical eye. "I think it looks perfect. The binding around my chest is a tad too tight." She squirmed, uncomfortable. "But overall, I think I'll pass for a man."

She was taller than most women. For once, her height was an asset.

Bernadette sighed. "I'll loosen it a bit, but you do have breasts, Gabrielle. You are a woman. For God's sake, you're a princess wearing men's clothing. This mad plan of yours has me worried sick."

"Everything will be fine." Gabrielle removed the blue satin justacorps she wore and handed it to Caroline. She fumbled with the closures on her breeches a bit before opening them and pulling out the shirttails.

Her plan had her more than a little anxious, too, but she refused to show her unease to her two closest confidantes, her ladies-in-waiting. Both distant cousins, they were a few years older than Gabrielle and the only ones she trusted to take with her on this secret trip from the Palace of Versailles to Paris.

The only ones she'd divulged her true intentions to. There were only three people she trusted in the world, her half brother Daniel and the two women before her.

"Hold up your arms," Bernadette said, slipping her hands under the shirt and loosening the binding around Gabrielle's breasts. "There, is that better?"

Gabrielle took a deep breath. "Much better." She readjusted her clothing and accepted the justacorps Caroline handed to her.

"What if the King realizes you're not in the country with your uncle at his château?" Bernadette asked.

"Never mind that." Caroline waved off Bernadette's comment. "What if His Majesty learns you stole some of the royal diamonds and intend to gamble them at the *Basset* table? He's put a ban on the game." She shook her blond head. "I don't even want to think about what he would do!"

"The King has done nothing to enforce the ban. And as for the diamonds, I didn't steal them. I'm borrowing them. Stealing implies I intend to keep them. I don't," Gabrielle said. "They'll be returned once I win enough to cover Daniel's debt." Listening to Caroline carry on only spiked her fears. She knew what she was doing was risky, but what choice did she have? "I'll not abandon him. He is barely seventeen and they took advantage of him."

Her half brother was not in the habit of gambling. He was coaxed and bamboozled into it, and it infuriated her.

"At seventeen, he is a man, has been a man for two years now. He should have known better than to gamble and lose a vast fortune—at an *illegal* game," Caroline argued.

"There are those twice his age, and older, who have been lured to the Basset tables," Gabrielle countered. She adored Daniel and was crushed when her mother, who had once been the King's mistress, passed away. She'd lost her mother and Daniel in the same week. He was removed from the palace—sent to live with his father's family. The King having legitimized all his illegitimate children from his many mistresses had lost interest in her mother once Gabrielle was born. She'd married the Baron de Leclerc, Daniel's father, shortly thereafter, but sadly he'd died within the first year of their marriage.

The King had permitted Daniel and her mother to remain at the palace, close to Gabrielle, but once her mother was gone, her beloved brother was torn from her. He was only eight.

They'd been inseparable until then.

She wrote to him constantly. Worried about him always. Missed him madly, for she rarely saw him.

When he came to her last week and told her what had happened at the Duc de Navers's Hôtel, Gabrielle was devastated for him.

He was in financial ruin. He couldn't pay his servants. Couldn't maintain his château.

She refused to see him financially destroyed. It was difficult enough seeing him so heartbroken and dispirited. Daniel would do anything for her. No matter what. She, in turn, would do anything for him. Including taking some of the Crown gems and using them to win back Daniel's fortune.

"I'll not see my brother destitute, Caroline." Gabrielle picked up the periwig off the bed and placed it over her hair. If she didn't help him, no one else would. No one in his father's family or on her mother's side would wish to cover his gambling debt. Especially one so sizable.

And the King had never cared in the least about Daniel.

Bernadette swiped an errant curl from her cheek, her dark hair a sharp contrast to Caroline's fair coloring. "We don't wish to see him destitute either. We're just . . . well, we're most concerned about your scheme."

"I know you are." Gabrielle placed her hand on Bernadette's shoulder. "But I am no novice at Basset. I've played many times at court with His Majesty and the courtiers—until the King banned the game. I'll do fine." She was far better than most. "I'm not without wit and luck," Gabrielle added.

One didn't survive the politics and intrigue at court without having a good dose of both.

Or without being resourceful and clever.

Gabrielle had fooled His Majesty into believing she was visiting with her uncle. Fooled her uncle into allowing her the use of his private townhouse in the city while he was at his château. With no funds at her disposal—for members of the royal family didn't carry coin—she'd thought of a solution and slipped away from the palace with a pouch of diamonds. She'd even managed to turn her entourage of musketeers back to the palace without raising suspicion.

Trickery and deception weren't things she liked. But they were part of her world and deeply entrenched in the royal palace.

Being a convincing liar was more than an essential asset at court.

Her skills in dupery were finely honed after her mother's death. Only then, when she found herself alone in the palace without her mother's protection, did she learn just how much her mother had shielded her from. Duplicity hadn't come easy to her at first. Her conscience had weighed on her in the beginning.

Now she was numb to it.

Besides, desperate situations required desperate measures.

She had two weeks.

Clearly, luck was on her side; she'd made it to her uncle's townhouse in Paris. From here she had easy access to the Duc de Navers's gaming den at his Hôtel—and what amounted to four nights of Basset.

If she was to succeed in recouping Daniel's losses and not lose the diamonds she'd gamble with, luck had to remain on her side.

She couldn't—wouldn't—fail. Nothing would get in her way.

THANK YOU for reading THE LOVELY DUCKLING!

Want my next release for just **99¢?** Sign up for my **99¢ New Release Alert** newsletter at www.LilaDiPasqua.com. Each new release will be **99¢** for a SHORT time only. Get notified. Don't miss out!

FIERY TALES SERIES

Novellas
Sleeping Beau
Little Red Writing
Bewitching in Boots
The Marquis's New Clothes
The Lovely Duckling
The Princess and the Diamonds

Holiday Novella
The Duke's Match Girl

Anthologies
Awakened by a Kiss
The Princess in His Bed

Full-length novels
A Midnight Dance
Undone
Three Reckless Wishes

Lila DiPasqua is a *USA TODAY* bestselling author of historical romance with heat. She lives with her husband, three children and two rescued dogs and is a firm believer in the happily-ever-after. You can find her on Facebook, Twitter, Instagram, and Goodreads!